The Cat Sitter and the Canary

The Cat Sitter and the Canary

A Dixie Hemingway Mystery

BLAIZE AND JOHN CLEMENT

MINOTAUR BOOKS

A Thomas Dunne Book

New York

A THOMAS DUNNE BOOK FOR MINOTAUR BOOKS.
An imprint of St. Martin's Publishing Group.

THE CAT SITTER AND THE CANARY. Copyright © 2016 by Blaize and John Clement. All rights reserved. Printed in the United States of America. For information, address St. Martin's Press, 175 Fifth Avenue, New York, N.Y. 10010.

www.thomasdunnebooks.com
www.minotaurbooks.com

Library of Congress Cataloging-in-Publication Data

Names: Clement, Blaize, author. | Clement, John, 1962– author.
Title: The cat sitter and the canary : a Dixie Hemingway mystery / Blaize and John Clement.
Description: First Edition. | New York : Minotaur Books, 2016. | "A Thomas Dune Book."
Identifiers: LCCN 2016030748 | ISBN 978-1-250-05117-2 (hardcover) | ISBN 978-1-4668-5203-7 (e-book)
Subjects: LCSH: Hemingway, Dixie (Fictitious character)—Fiction. | Women detectives—Florida—Fiction. | Pet sitting—Fiction. | BISAC: FICTION / Mystery & Detective / Women Sleuths. | GSAFD: Mystery fiction.
Classification: LCC PS3603.L463 C378 2016 | DDC 813/.6—dc23
LC record available at https://lccn.loc.gov/2016030748

Our books may be purchased in bulk for promotional, educational, or business use. Please contact your local bookseller or the Macmillan Corporate and Premium Sales Department at 1-800-221-7945, extension 5442, or by e-mail at MacmillanSpecialMarkets@macmillan.com.

First Edition: December 2016

10 9 8 7 6 5 4 3 2 1

For Mom

Acknowledgments

As always, my deepest gratitude goes first to my editor, Marcia Markland (this time perhaps a little deeper, if that's even possible), for her guidance and patience; thanks also to the rest of my team at St. Martin's Press/ Minotaur, including assistant editor Quressa Robinson, senior marketing manager Martin Quinn, and copy editor Angela Gibson. Thanks also to Dana Beck for saving the rabbit from a certain death-by-celery; to Hellyn Sher for preventing me from rearranging the Florida Keys; to William McNeil for the title; to David Urrutia for his perseverance; to Detective Chris Iorio and the men and women of the Sarasota Sheriff's Department; to Al Zuckerman, my agent, for offering to loan me money; and finally to all of Dixie's fans and readers, who've welcomed me with hearts wide open.

Hope is the thing with feathers
That perches in the soul,
And sings the tune without the words,
And never stops at all
                    —Emily Dickinson

The Cat Sitter and the Canary

1

I don't like surprises.

In fact, I'm a lot happier when things are downright predictable . . . *boring* I guess is the right word. Not that I've always been like this. Once upon a time I was as carefree and breezy as the next idiot, rolling with life's punches like a champion fighter. But a girl can only take so many hits before she starts to go a little nuts, so if you'd prefer to stay on my good side, don't jump out of the closet and scare me, don't surprise me with a birthday party, and for the love of God, don't come knocking on my door without calling first.

I'm Dixie Hemingway, no relation to you-know-who. I live on Siesta Key, a little tadpole of an island that shimmies off the shore of Sarasota, about midway down the west coast of Florida.

In summer, when the sun drapes herself over our shoulders like a bear rug, we've got fewer than six or seven thousand permanent residents. But in season, while the rest of the country is avoiding overhanging roofs for fear of falling icicles, we're wearing flip-flops and drinking cervezas down on the beach. That's when our population swells to more than twenty thousand. We call them snowbirds. They come (with pets in tow) from all over the world to warm their weary, frost-nipped wings and relax with a daiquiri or two (or three) on one of our world-famous beaches.

It's hard to imagine how our little island stays above water with all that extra weight, and us locals like to complain about the traffic and the tourists stepping out into the road like they own the place, but in truth it keeps our economy in the black. Besides, we've got a constant sea-kissed breeze floating through the palm fronds, dolphins playing in the clear blue ocean, and blooming bougainvillea scenting the air with just the slightest hint of honeysuckle. Who could ask for more?

I always say I'm a cat sitter because that's how it started, but really I'm a *whatever* sitter. I'll happily take care of whatever you've got: dogs, hamsters, parrots, fish, ferrets, iguanas—all God's creatures, great and small.

Except snakes. If somebody calls up with a pet snake they need looking after, I try to keep my voice at a normal volume and politely refer them elsewhere. It's not that I hate snakes, there's just something about dropping little squirming mice into a snake's open mouth that gives me the creeps. Plus, I'm not so sure it was God that came up with the whole idea of snakes in the first place.

I used to be a deputy with the Sarasota Sheriff's Department. I wore a gun on my hip and a five-pointed star on my chest. I patrolled the streets in my cruiser like a blond badass. Or at least that's what I told myself. In those days, things were pretty quiet around here. We had our share of criminals (what tourist town doesn't?), but all in all, it was a pretty quiet life.

It's funny, since I left the force and became a cat sitter, things haven't always been so quiet . . .

The sun was starting to set by the time Charlie and I turned down Old Vineyard Lane and rolled to a stop in front of Caroline Greaver's house. Charlie is a nine-year-old, fluffy-faced Lhasa apso who thinks he's a much bigger, more athletic breed—like a greyhound or a German shepherd. Charlie's humans, Otis and Deborah Weber, are a retired couple from Ontario who live on Bird Key, our smaller, fancier sister island just north of here. They're big-time animal lovers, so the first thing they did when they moved here was drive over to the local pet shelter and ask for the dog nobody else wanted.

That's how they got Charlie.

He's a good boy, but before the Webers came along he'd been adopted seven times, shuttled in and out of seven different homes, with each new owner telling the shelter that he was just too destructive to be left alone. The Webers were volunteering at the Women's Exchange, a giant consignment shop that donates all its proceeds to local charities and art programs, so Charlie was accompanying me on my rounds for the day.

Just as I reached into the backseat to unhook his harness, Charlie's back went stiff as a board, and he let out a low, rumbling growl. I looked up to see a woman two houses down. She was untying a couple of balloons—one forest green and the other bright yellow—from the lamppost in front of her house, but then I realized it wasn't the woman Charlie was growling at.

There was a man standing at Caroline's front door.

He was tall and broad-shouldered, in an expensive-looking three-piece suit and tie, holding a giant suitcase with one hand and a slim black briefcase in the other. I got out of the car and shut the door before Charlie jumped into the driver's seat and barked in protest.

I said, "Hi, can I help you?"

The man flashed a big-toothed smile and then ambled down the driveway, dragging his big suitcase behind him.

He said, "Ingrid?"

"No, I'm the cat sitter."

"Oh." He frowned. "There's nobody home. I tried to call ahead but there was no answer."

He had a thick Scottish brogue, so thick in fact that it took me a second or two to understand him. He was obviously speaking English, but what he'd said sounded more like, *"Eh troy to cull a hate, bother was naw ants uh."*

He was as handsome as a cliché: late thirties or early forties, with curly, unkempt hair, dark brown except for an even sprinkling of premature silver, and eyes a deep black. The first thing I thought was that if they held a Mr. Scotland beauty contest somewhere, he'd be the winner in a heartbeat.

"Do you know if she's home?"

I glanced up at the house. Caroline was away with her new boyfriend on a boat tour of the Florida Keys.

I said, "Was she expecting you?"

"Uh-oh." He pulled a piece of paper out of his breast pocket and deftly unfolded it with one hand, holding on to his briefcase with the other. "I think I've made a mistake. Is this 17 Old Vineyard Lane?"

"No," I said, pointing to the house across the street. "Seventeen's right there. This is fifteen."

"Ah, then. That explains it. I lost my glasses at the airport. I'm a right blind bat without 'em." He held the note out to me. "That *does* say 'seventeen,' yeah?"

The address was scrawled in thin blue ink on what looked like a page torn from a doctor's prescription pad. There was embossed print near the top, but the man's thumb was in the way so I couldn't make out what it said. In the lower left corner was a neatly drawn heart around the initials "IK" in the same scratchy handwriting.

"Terrible penmanship, right?"

I smiled. "I've got perfect vision and I can barely read it myself, but yes, it does say 'seventeen.'"

He folded it back into his pocket as his eyes swept down my body. "Sorry about that. *Rot gnome bah, rung hoss.*"

Charlie had clambered into the cargo hold and was watching us from the rear window.

The man flashed me another smile. "Cat sitter, eh? I bet that's an interesting profession."

"Sometimes." I tried to look as friendly as possible, but I was beginning to get a weird vibe from the guy, and

I think it's safe to say that Charlie was too. Just then he let loose with a barrage of vicious-sounding barks.

The man said, *"Furry boots?"*

"Huh?"

He waved one hand in the air like he was erasing a chalkboard. "Sorry. I keep forgetting I'm not in Scotland. Where from?"

"Oh. Right here. Born and raised."

He leaned over and peered into the back of the Bronco, his nose just inches from the window.

"And who's your buddy?"

Charlie responded by lunging at the glass and gnashing his teeth. The man barely flinched. He just nodded approvingly and muttered something that sounded like, *"Hats a rot goad bay."*

I said, "He's not normally so rude."

He winked at me. "Well, pretty little thing like you, I don't blame him. He's just protectin' his *booty*."

For a split second I tried to figure out what word in the English language sounded the most like "booty," but then the smirk on the man's face told me there was no translation needed. Slowly, I put my hands on my hips and took a deep breath. I've been known to have a bit of a temper. I don't take kindly to perfect strangers referring to me as a *thing*, or, for that matter, as anyone's *booty*. In fact, there was a time, and not so long ago, when a remark like that would have resulted in a little lunging and gnashing of my own.

"Rupert Wolff."

He was holding out one hand and grinning. "With two *f*'s. The second *f* is for *frrriendleh*."

I like a man with a firm handshake, but I never found out if Mr. Scotland's grip was firm or not. I looked down at his black patent-leather shoes, polished to a mirrored perfection, and then I noticed his perfectly manicured nails.

I thrust my hand out and said, "Well, I've been cleaning litter boxes all day, so . . ."

His eyes widened. "Oh, have you then?"

I shrugged, "Yeah. My husband's a little grossed out by it, but what can you do? Comes with the profession. And anyway, a little cat poop never killed anybody. Not that I know of."

He withdrew his hand slightly. "Yes, I suppose so. Well, don't let me keep you. We'll meet again, yeah?"

Before I could even answer he turned on his heels, grabbed his suitcase, and made a beeline for the house across the street.

I congratulated myself as I pulled Charlie's leash out of the backseat and snapped it on his collar, but I wasn't happy about Charlie's behavior one bit. I considered giving him a lengthy lecture about the dos and don'ts of proper dog etiquette, but given Mr. Scotland's less-than-stellar behavior, I figured Charlie was probably just trying to protect me.

He looked up and blinked, as if to say, *You're welcome*, and then launched another couple of warning *woofs!* in Mr. Scotland's direction.

I would normally have gone in Caroline's front door, but I didn't want Charlie making any more noise, so we took the quicker route to the side entrance—a small covered portico with two whitewashed benches on either side and a big terra-cotta urn for umbrellas. The key I had only worked the front door, but luckily I remembered Caroline kept a side key hidden on the ledge over the door. I dropped my backpack down on one of the benches and ran my hand along the ledge, and without even thinking I let go of Charlie's leash. In a flash he took off through the cat door, dragging his leash behind him like the tail of a runaway kite.

I unlocked the door as fast as I could.

Charlie had already raced down the long hallway toward the living room, and I could hear his high-pitched barks and something else that sounded suspiciously like scratching.

I rushed through the house yelling, "Charlie! No!" But it was too late. He was up on his hind legs at the other side of the living room, clawing at the door that opens to the front entry like a harp player on speed. I swooped him up in my arms and looked down at the door with a sigh.

There were scratches all along the bottom where his little nails had dug into the paint. I shook my finger in his face and said, "Bad!" as firmly as possible, but he just blinked and then licked the tip of my finger.

Like I said, he's a good boy.

I slipped the end of his leash through my belt loop and tied it in a knot, and then I marched him back through the living room. For a split second, I thought about opening that scratched-up door to see what in the world he was so interested in, but I knew it would be pointless. Sometimes, there's just no rhyme or reason to Charlie's antics.

That turned out to be a pretty good decision on my part—not opening the hall door—because if I had, I might've discovered what was waiting for me on the other side.

Instead, I got to remain blissfully ignorant for just a little while longer . . .

2

You need one of those kooky, made-up words to describe Caroline's house . . . like *fantabulous* or *increderrific*. It's an old Victorian, probably built around 1920. The outside looks like an antique dollhouse, but the inside is a mishmash of modern, antique, and traditional. Somehow, though, it all fits together perfectly. A big grand piano stands court over a leather Barcelona sofa, flanked on either side by two overstuffed armchairs upholstered in brightly colored rugs from India, each accompanied by a gooseneck floor lamp with beaded shades, and then there are sculptures and paintings practically everywhere you look.

There was no sign of Caroline's cat, though. He's a mackerel tabby, meaning his coat consists of contrasting colors that run along his shoulders and down his sides like a pinstripe suit—except in Franklin's case, the stripes are almost invisible. His fur is a light cream, lined with delicate bands of pale beige, like dried seagrass lying across a sand dune. Add to that his luminous avocado-green eyes and you've got one very handsome young man. Of course, I mostly know all this from the framed photographs on Caroline's piano. In the dozen or so times that I've taken care of him, I've only laid eyes on Franklin about twice.

He's a loner, which, as anyone with cats can tell you, isn't all that unusual. Franklin, however, takes it to a whole new level. As long as he's got fresh water and a full bowl of kibble, he's perfectly content. His favorite place to spend the day is on the back of the couch in the living room, where he has a view out the window and can watch the activities in the front yard and the street beyond, but by the time I get there he's already headed for one of his hiding places. If I'm lucky, I catch a glimpse of his tail disappearing around the corner down the hallway.

I've tried to win him over with some of my most irresistible treats—a cube of cheddar cheese, some tuna jerky—but so far I've failed miserably. Except for Caroline, Franklin has absolutely no use for human beings.

I don't blame him. I feel the same way sometimes.

Luckily for me, Caroline still needs the services of a pet sitter, because Franklin isn't the only furry creature living under her roof. Before we went into the family room, I kneeled down in front of Charlie and leveled him with as serious an expression as I could muster.

I said, "Now, listen. I'm not sure you've ever met a rabbit before, but you need to know they can be very skittish."

He wagged his tail enthusiastically.

"So if you can't be polite, you'll have to wait in the car

all by yourself, and nobody wants that because you'll probably rip the whole thing to shreds."

He looked back over his shoulder toward the front of the house and sniffed the air. I think he was still thinking Mr. Scotland was looming nearby, so I tapped him gently on the top of his snout to get his attention.

"Got it?"

He cocked one ear and then wagged his tail again.

"Okay, let's go."

About a year ago, Caroline called me up to ask if I had any experience catching stray cats. It was well past midnight. She'd been down at the bar at Colonel Teddy's, and walking home she'd spotted what she thought was a kitten running across the street. She followed it around the back of the hardware store only to discover a tiny, terrified rabbit, wedged in a corner behind a stack of wood pallets and concrete pavers. By the time I showed up, the poor thing was so exhausted it practically surrendered itself. All I had to do was put my cat carrier down and it hopped right in, no questions asked.

You don't see them that often because they're so shy, but lots of wild rabbits live on the Key. I had just assumed Caroline's rabbit was one of them, but one look and I knew something was wrong. It had white fur as pure as snow, with downy beige ears and chocolate patches on its head and rump—not at all like our local rabbits, whose fur more closely resembles the splintery gray wood of a fishing pier. This particular little girl was most definitely *not* wild. In fact, I got the distinct impression that Caroline's new friend had probably been purchased in a pet shop for Easter and then set "free" when the novelty wore off.

We named her Gigi, after the old movie with Leslie Caron and Maurice Chevalier, and that night Gigi slept curled up on the pillow in the curve of Caroline's neck. We had decided the vet should probably have a look just to be on the safe side, so the next morning Caroline called from Dr. Layton's office to report a clean bill of health and also to let me know that Gigi—she had just been informed—was a *boy*.

The name stuck, though. By then they were in love, and now wherever Caroline goes—restaurants, bookstores, shopping malls, you name it—Gigi goes with her, riding around in a vintage handbag with his little head and furry ears poking out the front. One thing about rabbits, though, they're not too crazy about boat trips, so Caroline had hired me to take care of him while she was away.

Gigi's cage—or rather, *mansion*—is situated on a specially built platform. The outside walls are painted to mimic the same wood-paneled facade of Caroline's house, with the same arrangement of windows, each with a tiny pair of curtains behind real glass, and it has the same domed cupola on the peak of its tile-covered roof, in miniature of course, with a tiny widow's walk running around it. There's even an itsy-bitsy weather vane perched on top. And just like Caroline's front door, Gigi's door is lacquered a deep Chinese red and flanked on either side with little brass lamps that actually turn on. Spaced evenly along the front porch are three fluted columns that rise all the way to a balcony along the second floor.

The only difference between Gigi's mansion and Caroline's, other than the size, is that Gigi's outside walls are all on hinges, so they can be folded open like louvered shutters to reveal the more conventional wire cage inside.

Of course, Gigi's place doesn't have a grand piano or paintings on the walls, but it has three levels, with a series of raised platforms that Gigi can play on, and there's even a little raceway that goes right through the wall behind the cage to the sprawling pool patio outside. It's all enclosed in a huge screened lanai, so Gigi can lounge around in the fresh air or explore the garden whenever he wants without having to worry about hawks or owls or alligators.

It's a good life for a rabbit . . . or anybody for that matter.

I led Charlie up to the cage, steeling myself for what I was sure would be a tense introduction. I pulled his leash taut and whispered, "Now, remember, behave yourself."

He gave me a wary look, as if to say, *"Don't I always?"*

I had assumed that as soon as Gigi laid eyes on Charlie, he'd run and hide, but I couldn't have been more wrong. He sat up on his hind legs, waggled his whiskers, and then hopped forward to say hi. He wasn't the slightest bit perturbed and neither was Charlie. He acted as if he'd known Gigi for years, although I had a sneaking suspicion he was more preoccupied with Mr. Scotland than anything else. He kept glancing over his shoulder toward the front of the house.

I opened up Gigi's cage and gave him a couple of scritches between the ears, and then moved him upstairs to his little balcony. I took out all the old bedding from his living room, wiped everything with a warm soapy washcloth, and then laid down a layer of newspaper, a sprinkling of wood shavings, and a fresh bed of timothy hay.

When I was done, Gigi came down the steps to evaluate my progress, and then I repeated the whole shebang on the upper floors while he set to work sculpting a nest-shaped bed out of the hay. Nobody had asked me to clean out Gigi's cage, but I didn't mind doing it. Just like humans, rabbits are a lot happier when their home is nice and tidy. We worked as efficiently as a professional housekeeping crew, and less than five minutes later the cage was as clean as a whistle and Gigi's bed was perfectly formed.

I washed my hands in the powder room in the hall, and then we all went out to the lanai. I let Charlie off his leash so he could go exploring, and Gigi and I stretched out on one of the lounge chairs by the pool to munch on some sweet potato slices I'd brought along for the occasion.

At some point, I remembered the mail. Caroline had asked me to gather it up every day and leave it in a basket she keeps on the hall table. There's no mailbox—everything goes through a brass-framed slot in the front door—and I remembered the last time I took care of Gigi the amount of mail that piled up on a daily basis was astounding, especially the catalogs. There must have been five or six a day, all full of the kinds of things I don't normally give a flip about (or admit to): fancy watches, expensive designer gowns, resort spas, and priceless jewelry.

But I decided it could all wait. I wasn't exactly sure when Caroline was coming back—she'd said it would be no longer than a week but she'd let me know. And anyway, we were all enjoying ourselves and I didn't want it to end. Gigi was still on my lap, and Charlie was intently watching a lizard that had scampered up the outside of the lanai. I laid back and closed my eyes, listening to the sound of Gigi gently munching on his sweet potato while the birds and crickets sang the sun down.

Then I fell asleep.

One of the perks of being a pet sitter is that I can sometimes make it through an entire day without talking to a single human being. Not that I'm a social recluse or anything. Not anymore. I just feel more comfortable in the company of animals.

There's a downside, though.

Rubbing elbows with the animal kingdom on a daily basis means life can be a bit of a minefield: you never quite know what's around the corner (or what you might be stepping in). A perfectly well-trained dog might decide to race out the door for an impromptu meet and greet with the neighborhood, or an otherwise rationally minded feline might decide the living room curtains would be much nicer with a little fringe at the bottom. It keeps me on my toes, and it's never boring, and most of the time I feel like I'm pretty good at avoiding surprises.

But not always . . .

It felt like I'd only been lying there for a couple of minutes when I thought I heard someone call my name. I opened my eyes to find Gigi stretched out next to me, sound asleep, and Charlie curled up at my feet and snoring quietly. The sun had completely descended. The only light came from the swimming pool, and it took my eyes a couple of seconds to adjust to the darkness. I realized I must have been dreaming, and what I'd heard was probably just my inner voice telling me to wake the hell up.

But then I heard it again.

"Miss Hemingway?"

This time Charlie shot up and fixed his gaze on the row of tall shrubs that separates Caroline's place from the house next door. I didn't know what else to do, so I opened my mouth to say, "Yes?" but then Charlie barked a high-pitched *yip!* and the branches in the middle of the hedge parted.

A man emerged, not much taller than five feet. In the pale blue light from the pool, he looked like a shadowy apparition, which made me wonder if I wasn't still dreaming, except a flood lamp flickered on—it must have been connected to a motion detector—and the entire patio filled with bright fluorescent light.

The man had a boyish face, with dark curly hair and olive skin. He said, "I'm sorry to disturb you, ma'am. My employer sent me."

"Your employer?"

He was wearing black dress pants and a fitted, white

dress shirt buttoned all the way up to his chin, which sported a neatly trimmed goatee.

"Are you Miss Hemingway?"

"Yes, but . . ."

"Ms. Kramer wishes to speak to you."

I sat up and shook my head. "Sorry. I'm a little confused . . ."

He looked back behind him and pointed to the house over the hedge. "I work next door. She asked me to speak to you about a pet-sitting position."

I was wondering how he knew my name or that I was even here, but before I could ask, Charlie hopped off the chair and scampered over to the side of the lanai, his tail wagging like a whirligig. The young man knelt down and put one hand up against the lanai screen. Charlie stood up and gave him some enthusiastic high fives from the other side.

The man chuckled. "Hello there, little man. What kind of dog are you?"

As I've said before, I don't care much for surprises, but I figured I needed to be as polite and professional as possible. I said, "He's a Lhasa apso. His name's Charlie."

He said, "Charlie! What a good boy. Are you a good boy?"

Charlie looked back at me and then danced a little jig on his hind legs as if he hoped to answer before I could.

I said, "When he wants to be. We just met the gentleman that's visiting across the street, and he didn't get near as nice a greeting as you are."

The young man stood up and nodded curtly, almost as if he'd suddenly remembered he was still on duty.

He said, "Ms. Kramer would like to speak to you if you have a moment. She wants to know if you are only a cat sitter, or do you take care of other animals as well?"

I hesitated. I hadn't ever met the woman who lived next door, but just like most people within a hundred miles of the Key, I knew her name . . .

Elba Kramer.

The first time I'd heard of her was about seven years earlier, when I was still a sheriff's deputy. A call had come in reporting a disturbance on the south side of the bay, just a little ways down from the dock at Hoppie's restaurant. There was a very fancy yacht moored there, and a couple of tourists had snuck up and started taking pictures of it, which normally wouldn't have been a big deal, except the tourists weren't so much interested in the yacht as they were the mostly naked couple that was canoodling on its upper deck.

The couple turned out to be local celebrities of sort. The man was Morton Cobb, a well-respected politician who'd made his fortune in computer software. He was in the middle of his second term in the Florida state senate, and the woman was his much younger wife, an attractive brunette who mostly stayed out of the limelight. Once they realized they were being photographed, Mrs. Cobb hid her face behind a sun hat and escaped to the yacht's lower cabin, but Senator Cobb jumped off the boat and ran up the dock with nothing but a towel wrapped around his waist, threatening the tourists with all kinds of bodily harm and legal action if they didn't hand over their cameras immediately, which of course they didn't. They just kept shooting away.

It was an ugly scene. When I arrived, the senator demanded I confiscate the cameras myself, and when I refused, telling him I had no legal right to do so, he was furious. I can still see his face, scorched red and breaking out in beads of perspiration, calling me all kinds of names I can't repeat in polite company. He even threatened to have me kicked off the force, and for a while I worried he might actually do it. But in the end, it was just an idle threat from a desperate man backed into a corner. The whole thing would probably have ended right there were it not for the fact that the next morning, strategically pixelated photos of the senator groping his topless wife were splashed all over the local newspaper.

Everybody had a good snicker about it, and the senator held a press conference later that day to denounce the shoddy morals of the tourists and decry the slipping standards of the local law enforcement, but it certainly didn't look like it was the end of his political career.

That came later.

About three hours later, to be precise, when a local television reporter spotted Senator Cobb's wife in Pensacola, where she'd been for two days, visiting her mother. Of course, that didn't make any sense, because Pensacola is a seven-hour drive away, and if the senator's wife had been there for two days, then who in the world was that topless brunette with the senator? Hiding her face behind a sun hat on the front page of the *Sarasota Herald-Tribune*...?

Yep, you guessed it... Elba Kramer.

She'd been a well-known model a decade earlier, so of course that just added fuel to the fire. The affair made headlines not just here but all over the country, effectively putting an end to the senator's dreams of one day living in the White House. From that point on Elba Kramer's name popped up in the news regularly: she was spotted at a Hollywood party on the arm of a married rock star, she was thrown out of a nightclub in Berlin for public indecency, she'd been accused of shoplifting in a tony jewelry store in London, and now she was married to a man forty years her senior, who just happened to be filthy rich.

All the locals followed the trajectory of her life with sanctimonious disapproval, which is why it wasn't long before the name Elba Kramer became synonymous with scandal. She was, as a letter to the editor later dubbed her, the Scarlet Woman of Siesta Key.

"Miss Hemingway?"

I blinked. Elba Kramer's assistant was still standing just outside the lanai, looking at me with raised eyebrows.

"Oh, sorry," I said. "What was the question?"

"Ms. Kramer wanted to know if you are only a cat sitter. She has a bird she would like your help with."

"Sure. I take care of all kinds of pets. What kind of bird is it?"

He tipped his chin up. "An intense yellow lipochrome."

I said, "An intense yellow who?"

"Lipochrome. Nonfrosted."

His demeanor was all business, and I got the distinct

impression that Elba Kramer took her bird very seriously. He glanced over his shoulder and then lowered his voice. "Perhaps you could follow me now. Ms. Kramer can give you the details."

I glanced down at my wrist, which was ridiculous since I haven't worn a watch in years. I said, "You know, I wish I could, but I didn't realize how late it is. I need to take Charlie home before his owners start wondering where he is. I'd be more than happy to come back any time."

"Perhaps tomorrow afternoon then? Ms. Kramer is available after five."

"That's perfect. I can be here by five thirty."

"Excellent. Let me give you the house number."

I opened the screen door, and he handed me a small business card, charcoal gray with fine white lettering. It read, RAJINDER LUXFORD, MANAGER followed by a telephone number.

He said, "That's the main house line. If there should be a change in your plans, you will please let me know?"

I nodded. "Of course."

He headed for the bushes but then stopped and looked back. "One more thing. Ms. Kramer requires the utmost discretion. I must ask that you not speak of her personal affairs to anyone, and she will require that you sign a nondisclosure agreement."

I gulped. "Oh."

"Will that be a problem?"

I felt a little jolt of guilty pleasure, the way you feel when someone starts to tell you a particularly juicy piece of gossip—some secret that's none of your business that they really shouldn't be sharing—and yet you find yourself completely incapable of telling them to stop.

I shook my head. "No. Not a problem at all."

Rajinder bowed politely and then disappeared back through the bushes. I looked down at Charlie, who was grinning at me and wagging his tail.

I'd always wondered what life was like for the infamous Scarlet Woman of Siesta Key. Now, apparently, I was going to find out.

3

When my radio alarm went off the next morning, I didn't get a chance to find out what song was playing. Instead, my arm shot out as if it had a mind of its own and slapped the snooze button. I was all tangled up in the sheets, and for a second I thought I'd use that as an excuse to sleep the morning away, but then I remembered I had a full day ahead of me. Normally I wouldn't have had to worry about traffic, but with all the tourists coming into town I knew if I didn't get a move on I'd never get to all my clients . . . which in my line of work would be a very bad thing.

I wriggled out of bed and padded naked down the hall. I can't sleep with clothes on, not even a T-shirt. I don't know why, but even a pair of ankle socks can keep me awake all night. If I'm ever forced to rush outside in the middle of the night, it'll be scandalous, but luckily the place is pretty secluded. It's above the detached four-slot carport next to the weathered two-story house I grew up in—the house where my brother, Michael, lives now with his partner, Paco.

We're right on the beach at the southern end of the Key, but the house is barely visible from the road. There's a crushed-shell driveway that meanders through a jungle of Australian pines, sea grape, mossy oaks, and palm trees, then it makes a turn to the left and edges along the beach. There's a rusty old sign at the entrance to let people know it's not for public access, but people nose down it anyway.

The property sits on a little blip of sandy shore that wanes and waxes with the tide, alternately eroding and rebuilding from year to year. That wavering property line makes our land just a tad less valuable than a lot of other properties on the Gulf (and keeps the property taxes hovering just above preposterous). But still, even though the house and my apartment aren't worth a hill of beans, the land they sit on is worth millions.

My place is tiny, which suits me just fine. There's a galley kitchen with a breakfast bar separating the living room in the front, and then there's a small bedroom at the end of a short hallway with a bathroom on one side, a laundry alcove on the other, and a big walk-in closet. A row of windows overlooks the balcony and the court-yard below, with metal storm shutters that I can close with a remote if there's a hurricane looming or if I just feel like having a little extra security.

I pulled open the french doors to the balcony and stepped out into the cool morning air. The sun was just beginning to peek over the treetops to the east, sending long rays of pale lemon light through the mist off the beach down below. I'd recently put a couple of gigantic staghorn ferns up on the wood-paneled walls flanking the door, and their long fronds were reaching out to catch the dew.

I leaned against the railing and closed my eyes, listening to the waves and letting the salty air fill my lungs, feeling it move all the way down to my toes. I love it out here. It's my favorite place in the world. There's a yellow wrought-iron ice cream table with two matching chairs just by the door, and then in the corner facing the ocean is a big hammock filled with pillows of every conceivable size, shape, and color. At the start of each day I try to take a moment and just breathe it all in. It helps me remember to enjoy life as it comes, to live in what the "woo-woo" folk call the *here and now* . . . to just be happy where I am.

Also, it helps me forget how I got here.

There were a couple of seagulls ambling around on the deck down below where we eat dinner most nights. They were probably hunting for crumbs or leftovers, but they looked more like mall guards doing an early-morning security check. I still wasn't completely awake, so at first I didn't notice that the white hush of the ocean had taken on another familiar sound, sort of like distant radio static. I thought maybe I'd forgotten to turn the radio alarm off, but then I realized it wasn't static at all: there was a car coming up the crushed-shell lane from the main road.

Tourist season doesn't officially begin until November, but the most eager snowbirds start arriving now, around mid-October, when it's just starting to get seriously cold up north. But it was far too early for tourists to be snooping about, and I knew Michael and Paco were both at work.

"No way," I whispered out loud.

But then, sure enough, there was a flash of chrome through the leaves and what looked like a giant green station wagon slowly making its way around the curve in the drive. I felt like a deer in the headlights.

Or, more precisely, like a butt-naked woman on her balcony.

I don't exactly make a habit of traipsing around outside in my birthday suit, but with Michael and Paco both gone I hadn't given it a second thought. Now, whoever was coming up the driveway had a clear view of my front door, and it was far too late to slip back inside without being spotted.

If it was Michael or Paco, I might have been a little embarrassed, but it certainly wouldn't have been the end of the world. Then the thought flashed across my mind: What if it was a client? Or maybe an old colleague from the sheriff's department? Or the meter man? All of those possibilities seemed unlikely given the hour, but there was no time to think, so I did what any reasonable person would have done in the same situation.

I dove for the hammock.

It wasn't really a station wagon. More like a tank. One of those huge suburban SUVs that people ferry kids and bags of groceries around in. Fixed to the hood just above the shiny chrome grill was a silvery logo: the letter *B*, with gleaming feathered wings sprouting from its sides.

The car rolled to a stop just shy of the deck, and as I

snuck one hand out and grabbed the railing to steady the hammock, the driver's side door swung open and out stepped a man in his midsixties, about six feet tall, with a nose like the beak of a hawk and eyes to match.

"Here we are!"

He was wearing standard rich-tourist couture: shorts the color of an easter egg (in this case bright yellow) and a white short-sleeved polo shirt with the collar flipped up jauntily.

The woman rose up and pivoted around on one foot like a ballerina popping out of a music box. She wore taupe jodhpurs and a white blousey dress shirt with rolled sleeves, and even at this distance, buried in pillows and peering through the ropes of the hammock, I could see the glitter of a diamond tennis bracelet on her wrist, along with matching diamond pendants hanging from her ears. Even her long, silvery blond hair looked expensive.

She said, "Garth, it's perfect."

"I know." He folded his arms over his chest and looked around. "I told you it was perfect. Didn't I say it was perfect?"

"You did."

I rolled my eyes, thinking of Christopher Columbus, all puffed up and congratulating himself on his new "discovery."

She said, "But then again, you say the same thing about every house we find, so you can't blame me for being a little dubious."

He snorted. "I can and I do."

I slunk down a little farther in the pillows and closed

my eyes, hoping it made me more invisible. I knew if they decided to come up the steps I'd be forced to reveal myself, so to speak, but they didn't seem one bit concerned somebody might be home. While the woman stepped up on the deck between the carport and the main house, the man walked under me. I could see the white of his shirt between the floorboards of the balcony as he snooped around my car.

"Edith, look at this old Bronco. We've got one of these down at the club. Belonged to Hank Patterson. You remember old Hank Patterson from Crown Oil?"

"God, no."

"Well, the story is he chatted up some girl at the bar young enough to be his daughter. Then she ended up driving him home because he was too drunk to drive. Well, don't ask me what happened next, but guess what happened next?"

She rolled her eyes. "Please, don't tell me."

"He walks through the front door and his wife is there, mad as hell. She says, 'Hank, where the hell is the Bronco?' And the bastard says, calm as rain, 'I donated it to the club.' And that was that! Now they use it to bring the pheasants down to the range."

The woman nodded as she drew a couple of stray hairs behind her ear. "That's a beautiful story."

He put his hands on his hips and scanned the line of the overhang that runs the length of the balcony. "Looks like they've got a renter up there. You know, if you tore this carport down, there'd be room for a cabana."

My eyes widened.

The woman sighed. "You mean a guesthouse."

"No, Edith. I mean a cabana. To go with the pool. Maybe even an outdoor kitchen—*à la belle étoile*. Who the hell needs a guesthouse anyway?"

She shrugged. "Well, it definitely needs a pool, but I'd say tear it *all* down and start over."

The man took a few confident steps toward the main house. "I'd say this is a hundred years old at least. They don't make 'em like this anymore. It's got charm. We could probably get it on a list of historical homes. That could jack up the value considerably."

The woman stepped off the deck and reached into the front seat of the car for her purse. "Ha. As far as I'm concerned, *charm* just means *dirty*. All that old wood and drafty windows. And Garth, who cares about value anyway? It's not like we're flipping it."

He said, "Well, tear it down then. Either way, it's all about location. That's the thing to think about."

She tipped her head to one side as she lit her cigarette with a tiny white lighter. "Well, you'll get no argument from me on that point."

"Refreshing."

I had pressed my face down into the hammock to get a better view, and it was starting to feel like the ropes were burning into my cheeks. The man came back around to the car's side and put one foot up on the runner board.

"Beachfront property, Edith. Doesn't get any better than that." He tipped his chin at the ocean. "Wanna go down there and check it out?"

The woman took one long drag of her cigarette and then flicked it across the driveway with a shrug. "*Meh*. You've seen one beach, you've seen 'em all."

At that point, naked or not, I was one millisecond away from rising out of the hammock like Godzilla from the sea and pelting them with a few carefully chosen epithets—if not a couple of wrought-iron ice cream chairs—along with a ten-second deadline to get the hell off my property. Luckily for everybody involved, they both got back in their stupid green tank and pulled out, leaving an invisible cloud of foul-smelling exhaust in their path.

I sat up out of the pillows and blinked.

Tear it down!?

Never mind the audacity, slithering around somebody else's house unannounced and uninvited, but the mere thought that they'd tear our house down—the house my grandparents bought when they were newlyweds, the house Michael and I grew up in after our father died fighting a fire and our mother ran off . . . At this point, this old house is like a member of the family. And we've lost enough family as it is. We'll never sell.

Not while I'm still breathing.

I made a mental note to try to remember everything those two old fools had said so I could tell Michael and Paco all about it when they got home. I had a moment of regret I hadn't flown off the balcony to let them know exactly what they could do with their plans for the future, but I'm sure they would have called the funny farm and reported a naked lunatic on the loose.

As it turned out, ending up tied to a bed in a mental

hospital would *not* have been the worst thing in the world. In fact, given what was waiting for me around the corner—or should I say, behind that door to Caroline's front hall?—a nice medicated rest would have been just what the doctor ordered.

4

As soon as the coast was clear and my early-morning intruders had moved on to their next potential demolition site, I streaked back inside. I was completely behind schedule now, but fortunately my morning routine is quick and simple. I can practically do it in my sleep. My feet were still damp from the misty air outside, so I tiptoed to the closet, careful not to slip on the terra-cotta tile.

Despite the fact that my apartment is small, my walk-in closet is big enough to hold a world-class collection of designer shoes and expensive haute couture. Instead, I've got a filing cabinet and a small desk in one corner. Pretty much every stitch of clothing I own fits on one six-foot rack.

There was a time when I had tons of clothes, although none of it was exactly what you'd call high-end—casual stuff for dinner with friends from work, vaguely sexy stuff for a standing Friday-night date, rugged stuff for running around with the kids at the playground . . . but things are simpler now.

As I pulled on my standard cat-sitter uniform—cargo shorts, white sleeveless T, and a pair of white Keds—I surveyed the stacks of bills and papers spread across my desk. One of the advantages of growing up in a sleepy beach town is that you develop a pretty laid-back attitude about most things, but when it comes to work, I run a very tight ship. In fact, I like to think I operate my pet-sitting business with the same discipline and dedication I brought to being a sheriff's deputy. I'm always prepared, I'm respectful and kind to everyone I meet (furry, feathered, or otherwise), and I keep a spiral notebook with detailed notes on every pet I've ever cared for—what medications they take, what their favorite snacks are, and what kinds of games they like to play. Filing, however, is not my strongest skill. In fact, I like to pretend I have a private secretary named Dammit.

I shuffled things around on my desk and muttered under my breath, "Dammit, when are you going to get this place organized?"

Usually Dammit just rolls her eyes and mutters, "Oh, don't have a cow. I'll do it later," but of course she never does.

I finally found my calendar under a collection of bills and cat-treat coupons and went over the day's schedule. There were my regular morning clients first and then the rest were all felines. The Webers were volunteering again at the Women's Exchange, but today they were only working the second shift, so I planned to swing by and pick Charlie up after I started my afternoon rounds. My final appointment of the day was reserved for the Scarlet Woman of Siesta Key.

The plan was to time my arrival at Caroline's about forty-five minutes early and then, once Gigi was taken care of, I'd stop in next door for a quick meet and greet. The only problem was that I'd forgotten to mention to Ms. Kramer's assistant that I'd have a deranged Lhasa apso with me. I didn't like the idea of bringing someone's dog to an initial meeting, especially a dog as unpredictable as Charlie, but there was nothing to be done about it now.

Downstairs, there was a giant pelican roosting on the handlebars of my bike. I felt bad making him move, especially since I could easily have taken the Bronco, but I wanted to enjoy the cool morning air while I could. I knew within a couple of hours the roads would be more crowded, plus the sun would be out and it would be way too hot for pedaling around all day.

With a little encouragement, the pelican hopped over to the hood of the Bronco and then watched me with an incriminating glare as I backed out and rolled across the courtyard and down the curving driveway. Normally, the sound of the bike's wheels on the crushed shell sends the parakeets in the treetops into a flutter, but my morning explorers had already woken them up, so everything was eerily still as I made my way down to the main road.

For the rest of the morning and into the afternoon, I felt just slightly off-kilter. Biking around town usually makes me feel free as a country cat, but it wasn't working this time. I still felt . . . I don't know . . . *nervous* isn't exactly the right word, but something close to it. All six of my morning clients had been perfect angels overnight—no accidents to clean up or destroyed houseplants to doctor—but still I felt a tiny bit of foreboding every time I took out my keys and unlocked another front door. Even a quick nap before my afternoon rounds was completely useless.

The temperature had risen as the day went on, plus I couldn't very well pedal around with Charlie in tow, so after my nap I left my bike at home and switched to the Bronco. Luckily, I'd left all the windows open from the night before so it wasn't a broiling inferno inside— more like a toasty oven. I cranked up the AC, and it cooled off nicely.

At the Weber's house, Charlie was waiting for me just inside the gate to the backyard, which was a good thing since it meant I didn't have to go hunting for him. As soon as he saw me coming up the side driveway, he ran to his little igloo doghouse on the porch and brought back one of the many stuffed toys he keeps there—this time a ragged yellow giraffe—and shook it at me tauntingly.

I unlatched the gate and tried to be firm. "No, sir. We've got work to do. I promise we'll play when we get home later."

He ignored that and ran around in circles while I pulled his leash off a peg by the back door, and then I ran around in circles trying to hook it onto his collar. Finally, I gave up and let him run ahead to the Bronco, where he waited by the passenger door with his giraffe in his mouth and his tail wagging excitedly.

Just like people, animals are a lot happier when they

have a purpose in life, and I was beginning to think Charlie was enjoying his part-time employment. For the rest of my afternoon stops, he kept himself on good behavior (relatively speaking), and it made me smile every time I thought of it. Elba Kramer wasn't the only one around here with her own personal assistant.

By the time we finally finished up with my afternoon clients and pulled into Caroline's driveway, I was thoroughly pooped and so was Charlie. He was stretched out on the passenger seat with his chin resting on his giraffe, held in place between his paws. I switched off the ignition and told him to stay put while I got his leash, but he just lifted his head and sniffed the air tentatively.

I gave him a quick shoulder rub. "I know, buddy. Being a cat sitter isn't as easy as you thought, huh? All we have to do is feed Gigi, then a quick meeting next door, and then we're done for the day."

At that he stood up and wagged his tail in agreement, although his expression seemed more curious than eager. As I got out of the car, I glanced across the street to see if there were any signs of Mr. Scotland, and, sure enough, there he was, sitting in one of the wicker rocking chairs on the front porch with a book in his lap. He was wearing tan shorts and a T-shirt now, and even from a distance I could make out the tanned muscles of his arms. With the setting sun streaking the sky pink and amber overhead, the scene looked like something from a sexy postcard or a romantic movie. A baseball cap shaded his eyes, so I wasn't sure if he was watching me, but as soon as I raised my arm to wave, he immediately waved back.

"Gid evenin' mess!"

I said, "Hi there. How's your vacation going so far?"

He flashed a white smile. *"Hay rot braw!"*

I smiled back and nodded, having no idea what the hell he'd said. Charlie pulled me all the way up the walk to Caroline's front porch, ignoring my halfhearted commands to heel, and the closer we got to the front door, the more determined he became. The driveway had been baking in the hot sun all day, so I figured it was probably still too hot for his little paws. Either that or he was looking forward to adding a few more scratches to that parlor door.

I said, "Charlie, don't even think about it. From now on, you're staying on leash."

But I don't think he even heard me. He was too busy sniffing around the doorjamb, holding his tail out straight like an English pointer's. I shook my head in admiration.

Lhasas aren't exactly known for their tracking abilities, so it's easy to forget that even a tiny puffball like Charlie has the same not-very-distant ancestor as every other dog in the world: the gray wolf. And, just like wolves in the wild, dogs have a sense of smell that borders on the supernatural. They can detect microbial disease in beehives, counterfeit DVDs in foreign shipments, elevated blood pressure in humans—even a tablespoon of sugar in an olympic-size swimming pool! It was no wonder Charlie could still sense that Mr. Scotland had been here. I figured that man's smug, oozing charm could linger for days.

Just then, as if to prove my point, Charlie let out a low, rumbling growl.

"Charlie!" I tugged at his leash to get his attention. "I promise you there's nothing to worry about."

I glanced up to see if Mr. Scotland was still watching, but he must have gone inside. I flipped through my keys until I found Caroline's, which was silver with a red rubber tag attached, and as I slipped it in the lock and turned the handle, Charlie surged forward, ready to rush in ahead of me.

I said, "Hold on there, Speed Racer."

I pulled him back a few feet and made him sit, and then while I held one hand in front of his snout like a school crossing guard, I reached back and pushed the front door open with my right foot. Just then, Charlie looked down at the floor behind me and ever so slowly began wagging his tail.

I froze.

Dogs use their tails to communicate all kinds of things, but I knew beyond a shadow of a doubt that the particular signal Charlie was communicating was, *"Hello, stranger."* I slowly turned and peered over my left shoulder. There, in the middle of Caroline's front hall, surrounded by a sea of envelopes and flyers and plastic-wrapped catalogs, was a man.

His back was flat on the floor and his legs were laid out straight, but his left arm was at an odd angle, almost as if it didn't belong to the rest of his body. He wore a light-blue, three-piece suit, with a green-and-yellow striped tie. There was a white silk scarf laid across his face, so I couldn't see whether his eyes were open or not. As I leaned in closer, I realized the envelopes and mailers around his head and shoulders were soaked in blood.

I glanced down at Charlie. "Stay."

I knelt down and touched my thumb and forefinger to the man's narrow wrist, then, as calmly as possible, I pulled the door shut and locked it. I walked Charlie down to the Bronco, put him in on the passenger side, and then walked around the back, glancing across the street. Mr. Scotland had disappeared. I got behind the wheel and put my backpack down on the floorboard, and then I reached for the car keys in the cup holder between the seats. I started the car and backed about four feet down the driveway.

Where the hell are you going?

I shook my head as I cut the engine and sighed. I had no idea. All I knew was that I wanted to be as far away from there as possible. I got out and walked back up to the porch so Charlie wouldn't hear, and then I pulled out my cell phone.

"911, what is your emergency?"

The operator's voice seemed eerily close, almost as if he was standing right over my shoulder.

I said, "My name is Dixie Hemingway. I'm at Caroline Greaver's house on Old Vineyard Lane."

"Old Vineyard Lane?"

"Yes, sir."

"And what's the problem?"

I took a deep breath.

The human body is an extraordinary machine, armed with all kinds of survival systems that automatically kick in when it senses danger. The moment there's any kind of injury, every cell in the body jumps into action, flooding the bloodstream with hormones and pain relievers, stopping digestion, opening the lungs' air-ways, narrowing vessels, conserving body temperature, and slowing blood flow to all the major muscle groups. It's a finely tuned orchestration of events designed to preserve the body's strength, giving it the best possible chance of survival.

But the man lying in Caroline's front hall . . . there wasn't a doubt in my mind. He was beyond resuscitation. I knew he'd been dead for at least twenty-four hours. It was the temperature of his skin. It was ice cold, and there was a stillness around him that seemed thick and impenetrable, as if some small invisible amount of energy had been permanently sucked out of the universe.

I said, "I'm the cat sitter. There's been a murder."

5

This may or may not come as a surprise to you, but I've encountered a dead body before—and we're not talking about anything that happened during my career as an officer of the law. We're talking about after. Being a pet sitter, I'm in and out of people's houses all day long, every day of the week, and there's barely a neighborhood on the Key that I don't cross through at least once on my rounds. Not that there's a lot of crime around here. But when there is, the chances are pretty good I'm nearby, which means I've stumbled upon more than my fair share of crime scenes.

Like, *way* more.

Immediately after I hung up with the emergency operator, I dialed Caroline's cell phone. I knew it was only a matter of time before news of a murder on the Key got around, and I didn't want her finding out where it had happened before I got a chance to talk to her. Also, I was hoping if I described the man's clothing, she might know who he was.

The phone rang once, and as I was trying to figure out the most gentle way to tell her what had happened, a tiny shock rippled up my spine. At that point, I think my instincts must have kicked in and snuffed out any of the panic I was feeling, because suddenly there was room in my addled brain for what I should have been thinking all along . . .

Gigi!

I ended the call before the second ring and dropped the phone down in the side pocket of my cargo shorts. Charlie was sitting behind the wheel watching me, and as soon as I opened the back door, he hopped up between the seats and wagged his tail excitedly.

"Sorry, buddy," I said as I rolled the back windows down a bit. "But not a chance. Trust me, I wish I could take you with me, but I just can't. You'll have to stay put and guard the premises."

Immediately the thought popped into my head that whoever was responsible for what had happened to the man in the foyer could still be inside the house, but I told myself only a complete madman would murder somebody in cold blood and then hang around to find out what happened next. Of course, only a complete madman would murder somebody in the first place, but I decided to leave that out of the equation.

By now the sun had sunk down behind the trees. At this time of evening, there'd be hard-core sun-tanners coming in from a long day at the beach, fairer-skinned folks gathering to watch the sun sink into the ocean, and gaggles of teenagers tooling up and down the boulevard, in and out of souvenir huts and ice cream shops, veering around elderly couples walking hand in hand, out for a spell under the stars before an early dinner. For a brief guilty moment, I wished Charlie and I could be there with them, strolling along, completely unaware of what was happening here.

Instead, I shook my head and looked up at Caroline's front door.

The only good thing about the whole situation was that I knew beyond a shadow of a doubt that Caroline's cat would be safe. At the first sign of an intruder, I knew Franklin would've bolted straight to one of his hiding places. He was more than likely secreted away in the back of Caroline's closet or under one of the beds in an upstairs guest room.

I pulled my chatelaine out with shaking hands and was just about to put the key in the door when I stopped myself.

I whispered, "This is insane."

I knew I'd already compromised things enough by putting my hands all over the doorknob, not to mention disturbing the mail on the floor around the body when I pushed the door open. I knew it would only make gathering evidence that much worse if I went sneaking around inside the house now, so I just stood there, one foot firmly planted on the ground and the other just barely pointed in the direction of the Bronco. Every cell in my body was telling me to get in the car and drive around the block until the police arrived, but I just couldn't.

Not without checking on Gigi first.

I went back to the car and got Charlie, which was probably not the smartest decision in the world, but I didn't want to leave him alone where I couldn't see him. I wrapped his leash several times around my wrist to shorten it, and then together we walked up the driveway. At the top, just before the turn to the front door, we headed to the right and slowly made our way along the side of the house.

As we passed the portico, the walkway narrowed to a pebbled path, hemmed in with a dense hedge of camellias so lush their glossy leaves brushed the side of the house, forming a darkened tunnel all the way back.

I could feel the blood pounding in my veins, and I think Charlie must have sensed it, because he stayed right at my side, quiet as a mouse. At the first window, the curtains were closed so I couldn't see in, but I was pretty sure it was the master bedroom. We continued on to the next window, and this time the curtains were held open with tassels, so I had a view inside. It was another small bedroom, probably originally meant to be a nursery. There was a small bed with a baby-blue comforter and a collection of stuffed animals piled up on the pillows, and opposite that was an antique walnut dresser with a giant, gilt-framed mirror mounted on the wall above it.

I was about to move on when I realized if I positioned myself just right, I could see out the doorway and down the open hall in the mirror's reflection. I inched a little bit closer to the window as the entrance to the family room came into view.

I had a clear line of sight through the doorway to Gigi's cage. I could see his red front door and the two miniature brass lamps on either side of it. I could see the yellow mounds of his bedding, and I could see his glass water bottle perched at the top of the stairway on the second level . . . but there was no sign of Gigi at all.

Even as I told myself to stay calm, I felt a scream forming at the base of my throat, and then the next thing I knew I was racing through the camellias toward the back of the house with the branches slapping my face and Charlie announcing our presence with a string of frantic, high-pitched barks. Now, whatever cover we'd had was completely blown, and if I happened to be right and there was somebody still inside, things were about to get very complicated.

Just as we came around the corner, I slid to a stop and gasped.

Gigi was sitting under one of the lime trees. Luckily, I had the presence of mind to remember the screen door to the lanai. I slid my hand down into the side pocket of my cargo shorts and felt around for one of the carrot sticks I'd brought, thinking I could use it to coax him out.

Unfortunately, Gigi had other plans.

As soon as he saw me, every bunny nerve in his bunny survival system must have kicked in, because he darted across the lanai and disappeared like a flash through the raceway to his cage.

Charlie was still barking at the top of his lungs trying to figure out what the heck was going on, and I was frantically trying to shush him when there was a faint click from above and the entire lanai filled with blinding white light from the security lamp. I felt like I was caught in a searchlight, and then, as if to confirm it, there came a faint crunching sound from behind, and I realized with a jolt that it was growing closer.

Somebody was moving down the pebbled path, headed straight for me.

Without even thinking, I pulled Charlie close, and in the instant it took to turn around and see the metal glint of a gun pointed at my face, all the options I would have had as a sheriff's deputy flashed before my eyes: my two-way radio, my canister of high-pressure mace, my baton, my .38 caliber pistol . . .

Instead, I screamed bloody murder.

6

It's funny what a scream can do for you when you're in grave danger.

First, if you do it right, your eyes clamp shut and everything goes dark. Next, your body shrinks into a tight little ball, like a turtle pulling into its shell, and then your mind goes completely and utterly blank. The result is pure oblivion: you can't see a thing, and all you can hear is the sweet high-pitched singing of your vocal chords in all their stunning glory. You become the literal embodiment of the Three Wise Monkeys—hear no evil, speak no evil, see no evil.

I don't know how long I was in that state of bliss—probably just a few milliseconds—and I wasn't sure whether I'd heard a gunshot or not, but luckily when I opened my eyes I didn't find God waiting for me at the pearly gates or angels floating around on clouds and playing harps, nor did I see a fork-tongued demon welcoming me to the underground. Instead, I found myself looking straight down the barrel of a 9 mm Sig Sauer handgun, which I recognized immediately as the standard-issue firearm for all deputies with the Sarasota Sheriff's Department.

The man standing in front of me had piercing blue eyes, one of which was lined up with the trigger of his pistol, the other squinted half-shut. He had blond hair cut close to his scalp, with a sharp nose and high cheekbones that in the harsh light of the security lamp appeared to be chiseled out of concrete. A single diamond stud twinkled from the lobe of his left ear.

His eyes widened. "What the . . . ?"

I said, "Morgan?"

"Jesus, Dixie, you nearly scared me to death!"

I tried to speak, but my throat felt like I'd swallowed glass, and that, combined with the fact that there were dogs barking in the distance from every direction, told me that I must have screamed loud enough to terrify the entire Key.

I bent over and put my hands on my knees to steady myself. "Sorry. You scared me too."

Deputy Jesse Morgan. He had joined the department not long after I left, but, given my talent for discovering crime scenes, we had met on several occasions since.

He lowered his voice to a whisper. "Dixie, what in hell's name are you doing? You have any idea how dangerous it is to be sneaking around out here?"

I nodded. I knew exactly how dangerous it was, and I felt a lot safer now that Charlie and I weren't alone. Deputy Morgan is one of the Key's only sworn officers, meaning he's trained and licensed to carry a gun. He's slimly built but muscled and tall, with broad shoulders and a sharp mind—exactly the type of guy you'd want around if there were any murderers hiding nearby.

He hissed, "You could've gotten yourself killed!"

"I know."

Given how much noise we'd made already, it seemed pointless to go on whispering, but I kept my voice down just in case. "I didn't have a choice. I was trying to check on the animals. If I can just get in there and . . ."

He held up one hand. "Hold on: 911 said you discovered a body."

"Yeah. He's just on the other side of the door. He's wearing a light blue suit, and he's got a scarf over his face, so I have no idea who he is."

"A scarf?"

"Yeah. Silk. It's lying flat across his face." I wanted to add, *like a death shroud,* but I figured he got the picture.

"And where's the homeowner?"

"She's on vacation in the Keys. I'm not sure yet when she's coming back, a week or so, but I'm taking care of her pets until then, and the thing is—they're still inside."

"Who's inside?"

"Her pets."

That didn't seem to faze him one bit. "What's the homeowner's name?"

"Greaver. Caroline Greaver."

"She live alone?"

"Yeah. She's only been gone for two days. I was just here yesterday and everything was totally fine—nothing suspicious or out of place or anything—but then the second I got here today, something seemed weird."

"Which door is he at?"

"The front door. Caroline didn't say she'd have any visitors or anything. As far as I know, I'm the only one authorized to be here."

Morgan's pistol was at his side, pointed at the ground, but now he slipped it into its holster. "Okay."

I said, "You know what? I'd keep that handy if I were you. There might still be somebody in there, and if there is, I have to get . . ."

He stopped me. "Wait. When you called 911, you said the body had been there for at least twenty-four hours . . ."

"It's a guess. There's no pulse and his wrist is cold as ice. But when I opened the door . . . I don't know. Something didn't seem right. I just had a really weird feeling somebody was still in there . . ."

"But did you see anybody?"

I shook my head silently.

"Anyone on the street when you arrived?"

"No, not that I noticed."

He lowered his chin to his chest but kept his eyes locked on mine. After a quick moment, he motioned me to follow.

"Okay. Let's go."

He turned and headed back down the walkway, talking under his breath the entire way. "First, let's get you out of here until I can get some backup on the scene. If there's somebody in there, I don't want you anywhere near this house. After that, I can do a search of the premises and make certain it's secure. You can leave your car where it is . . ."

His voice trailed away as he stopped and turned around.

I was about twenty feet back, still standing at the corner of the house with one hand raised limply in front of me, pointing in the direction of the lanai.

"Dixie, what are you doing?"

I whispered, "I can't leave."

"Why the hell not?"

"There's a rabbit."

"A what?"

"Gigi. Caroline's rabbit. I told you. He's still in there. He was just out by the pool, but when he saw me he ran back inside. There's a pet door that leads to his cage. Franklin's probably hiding, but I can't leave Gigi in there all by himself."

He frowned. "Franklin?"

"Caroline's cat."

He put his hands on his hips and cocked his head to one side. Without even looking at the pained expression on his face, I knew he was thinking I was a complete idiot. I also knew there was no way he was letting me inside that house until he knew it was safe. Not to mention the fact that every square foot of the property and every single thing inside was potential evidence—including, unfortunately, Gigi and Franklin—and I knew Morgan didn't want me disturbing anything until an investigator was on the scene.

He took a deep breath. "Listen, I guarantee you the moment we determine it's okay, you can go in and get your animals, but for now you're coming with me . . . by force if necessary."

I frowned. There was certainly no need for that kind of attitude, but then again anybody who knows me knows

I can be a little stubborn when I want to. Charlie was standing at my feet, panting, and I realized I must have scared the poor guy to death when I screamed. He'd been searching my face for answers, but now he glanced over at Morgan and whimpered.

I said, "Okay. Let's go."

I picked Charlie up and followed Morgan alongside the house and down the driveway. When we got to the sidewalk, I paused, expecting him to turn right and lead me down the block to wait around the corner, but instead he stopped at his green-and-white police cruiser and opened up the back passenger door.

I said, "No, it's okay. I'll just take Charlie and go down the street until backup arrives."

"Like hell you will. Get in."

I'd probably spent thousands of hours inside a squad car just like Morgan's, but always in the driver's seat, never in the back, trapped behind the steel mesh and bulletproof glass like a caged animal. The thought occurred to me that anyone watching from one of the neighboring houses would think I'd been arrested.

Morgan cleared his throat. "Dixie. Get in the car. *Now.*"

I held Charlie tight as I got in, and as soon as Morgan shut the door and looked up at the house, I knew what he was thinking. I'd been through the same six-week deputy training program he had, although probably a decade earlier, but I knew the basic rules couldn't have changed that much. Standard protocol dictates that in the event of a possible homicide, as long as there's no imminent danger or pressing reason to search the premises, all first-responding officers should wait on-scene until an investigative team arrives. It's a safety measure, but it also minimizes the very real risk of contaminating evidence.

But I also knew no decent officer would respond to the report of a dead body without first confirming beyond a shadow of a doubt that there was no chance of resuscitation. I could have described the porcine cast of the man's skin, or the odd angle of his thin arm stretched out next to his body, or the absolute stillness of the silk scarf laid over his face, but it would have been a waste of time.

We both knew he'd be a fool to take my word for it.

Morgan was still standing next to the squad car, looking slightly hesitant, and I wondered if he wasn't considering getting behind the wheel and backing down the block so he could go inside without my knowing he was bending the rules a bit.

He was just about to make a move when I tapped lightly on the window. "Deputy Morgan?"

He turned and glared. "What now?"

"It's locked," I said.

He glanced down at the car's handle. "Yes. I'm aware of that. It's for your own safety. I'll let you out as soon as I know the house is clear."

I shook my head and held up my ring of keys. "No. I mean the front door."

He blinked. "Oh."

He opened the door and took the keys, nodding silently and mumbling something that sounded like, *thanks,* and then shut the door again after I showed him which key was Caroline's. After that, I slumped down in my seat and put Charlie in my lap. He was trembling slightly, so I tried to rock him like you might comfort a baby. We both watched Morgan as he retraced our path back up the driveway to the front porch. At the big picture window by the front door, he paused and peered inside. Just then a woman's voice cut the silence. It was the dispatch operator coming through on the police radio in the front seat.

Her voice was a thin wail, almost like a siren. "Deputy Morgan, backup en route, ETA is three minutes."

I glanced up at Morgan. He pulled his radio out and then seconds later I heard his voice. "Ten-four. Standing by."

He took another step past the window as he clipped the radio back on his belt and withdrew his gun. Then, in one swift motion, he unlocked the front door and disappeared inside. Less than twenty seconds later he came backing out with his radio in his hand again.

His voice was softer now. "Lorraine, this is Deputy Morgan. Possible Signal 5 here. We're gonna need a 10-93. I repeat, 10-93."

I had forgotten most of the technical jargon and law-enforcement terms within three or four months of leaving the sheriff's department, but a few of them had stuck in my brain like mice in a glue trap. "Signal 5" is police code for homicide, and "10-93" means "send detective."

There was a burst of static from the radio and then a couple more voices on top of each other, both talking so fast I couldn't understand a thing, but finally the dispatch operator said, "Deputy Morgan, please describe the victim."

"Approximately a hundred forty pounds, five foot nine inches. Caucasian."

"Age?"

"Midthirties."

"Male or female?"

There was a pause, filled with nothing but blank space, and then I heard what at first I thought was more static, but then realized it was Morgan taking a deep breath. I glanced up at the porch again. He was leaning with one arm braced against one of the big pillars, his legs at a wide stance, his head hanging down.

He said, "Female."

7

I was still sitting in the back of the squad car, trying to keep myself calm, while the night sky all around me was ablaze with the flashing red-and-blue lights of emergency vehicles. I counted at least three deputy cruisers, an ambulance, a Sarasota police van, and two unmarked cars. A line of traffic cones had been set up at both ends of the street to keep the gawkers and local reporters at bay, but there must have been at least a dozen deputies and crime technicians milling around in front of Caroline's house.

Despite all that, Charlie was sound asleep, curled up on the black vinyl seat next to me, and if I hadn't thought people would think I'd finally lost my marbles, I would have curled up right next to him. In the thirty minutes or so we'd been waiting, he had completely exhausted himself, barking at every single person that got within ten feet of the car, and I had completely exhausted myself going over every conversation I'd had with Caroline leading up to her departure, trying to remember if she'd said anything ... anything that might shed light on what had happened.

The first thing I remembered was a phone call I'd gotten from her about two weeks earlier. She'd recently started seeing a man, an ophthalmologist, who was currently separated from his wife of twenty years, although Caroline didn't know all the details yet. They'd only been dating for about a month and a half, but he was, in Caroline's words, a *catch*—not particularly handsome, but kind, smart, and extremely successful. He had talked a lot about a small schooner he'd bought last summer and how he never had time enough to enjoy it, and on their last date he had suggested they take it out and sail down the coast together.

Her immediate impulse was to say yes, but she told him she'd have to think about it. At that point they'd been on less than half a dozen dates, so she had called to get my opinion. Was it too soon? Was it insane to agree to a romantic getaway with a man she barely knew?

Given the fact that I don't like boat rides any more than rabbits do, I told her of course it was insane, but the real question she needed to be asking herself was, "How much do you like him?"

I remembered her response exactly. She said, "Dixie, I think I love him."

I closed my eyes and laid my hand on Charlie's side. I could feel his chest rising and falling with each breath, and for a few desperate seconds I tried to think of nothing but the sensation of it.

"Well," I said. "I guess we know why you were scratching at that door yesterday."

He lifted his head and squinted at me for a moment or two, then laid his head back down between his paws with a sigh.

I nodded. "You're right. I should have listened."

Until then, I hadn't allowed the thought to actually form in my mind. It was too terrible. But now I couldn't avoid it. The words rose up inside me, almost as if I was whispering to myself: *Dixie, is it Caroline's body in that house?*

It couldn't be. It just couldn't.

First of all—the light-blue suit. In all the time I'd known her, I'd never seen Caroline wear a man's suit. Ever. And anyway, if she hadn't shown up for the boat trip, her new boyfriend would have thought something was wrong. He would have tried to call her. And when she didn't pick up, he would have been worried. He would have gone to her house, and if there was no answer he'd have left a note on the door. And if that hadn't worked he'd have gone to the police and reported her missing.

Right?

I grabbed my phone again and shook my head.

Normally, I get detailed contact information for every one of my clients. I write down where they're going and who they'll be staying with. I get hotel numbers, nearby relatives, neighbors, vet information—anything I can think of that might come in handy in the event of an emergency. I'm extremely diligent about it. I never make an exception.

Except with Caroline.

She wasn't staying in a hotel, so it hadn't even occurred

to me to get another phone number or any other kind of contact information. All I had was her cell, and now I was dialing it for what felt like the hundredth time.

Her voice was bright and cheerful. *"Hey there, I can't talk right now because I'm doing something fabulous, either that or I'm too lazy to get my butt off the couch and pick up the phone, but if you'll tell me something interesting, maybe I'll call you back. Ciao for now!"*

This time, I didn't even wait for the beep. I just hung up. I'd already left at least five messages, each of them a variation of basically the same thing: *Call me!* I hadn't been specific about why, just that it was important I speak to her as soon as possible. I knew if I told her what had happened she'd definitely think it warranted a call back, but I didn't want to leave a voice mail, and—I shuddered at the thought—I was beginning to seriously wonder if she'd ever hear it anyway.

I shook my head again. There was no point panicking . . . *yet*.

Just in front of me, parked in front of Morgan's cruiser, was an ambulance from Sarasota Memorial Hospital, which is only about a five-minute drive from here, and directly behind me was a walnut-brown Lincoln Continental with Florida State government license plates. Beyond that was a black, four-door SUV with a light dusting of pollen across its windshield.

Blocking the entire roadway to the right, its front grill parallel with the back door of the ambulance, was the Sarasota County mobile forensics unit, a big square van that, if you didn't know better, you'd think was an ice cream truck. But I knew better. The side panels were open, and two forensics examiners, both in white lab coats, rubber booties, and latex gloves, were pulling out a couple of black nylon supply packs from a wall of shelves.

There were so many flashing lights in the street that when I closed my eyes I could almost imagine I was in a nightclub, so that's exactly what I did. I pictured myself far, far away—maybe on an exotic Mediterranean island in an old seventies-style disco with a fog machine and an over-the-top light show. I imagined myself swaying in time to the mind-numbing dance music and sipping on some mind-numbing drink, like a mojito or a pisco margarita, or maybe just a bottle of vodka.

The only problem was that instead of pulsing music overhead, all I could hear was the incessant tick-ticking of the emergency lights on the rack mounted to the top of the squad car. Just then there was a tap on the window and I opened my eyes to find Deputy Morgan watching me through the half-open window.

He said, "I thought you might want to know we searched the house. There's nobody in there but a rabbit and a very shy cat. They're both fine."

"Okay, thanks. And any word . . ."

My breath caught in my throat. Until now, I'd managed to present a relatively calm exterior, but I didn't think I'd be able to say Caroline's name without losing it.

I said, "Have they identified the body?"

Morgan shook his head. "You can wait outside now if you want."

"That's okay. I'll stay here with Charlie. He'll get too wound up if I let him out of the car now."

"No problem. Just got a couple more things to finish up, and then the detective would like to speak to you."

I said, "I've been trying to get ahold of Caroline, but she's not answering."

He paused for a moment.

"Don't call her again."

I watched as he went back over to the bottom of the driveway where there was a group of EMTs and deputies. In the middle was a tall woman with a nest of sorrel hair piled in a frizzy heap on top of her head. I could hear her talking quietly, but I couldn't quite tell what she was saying. All the men and women gathered around were listening intently, including a lanky, awkward-looking boy in a red baseball cap. I figured he must have been a neighborhood kid that got past the police blockade, or maybe he'd been brought on scene by one of the deputies, maybe he'd seen something suspicious.

Suddenly, I remembered my meeting with Elba Kramer next door. I grabbed my phone to check the time and then fumbled around in my backpack for the business card her assistant had given me. I looked up just in time to see Deputy Morgan tip his chin in my direction, and the tall woman with red hair turned and looked at me. She gave a short nod to the group, and then they dispersed like a football team breaking out of a huddle. Two of the deputies began stringing up a roll of bright yellow tape with the words POLICE LINE—DO NOT CROSS written in ominous black letters, and another man started pulling out cameras and lenses from a green duffel bag on the hood of an unmarked car.

Deputy Morgan was headed straight for me.

I put my phone down and turned to Charlie. "Now listen, I don't want you barking at anybody while I'm talking to these people, okay?"

He lifted his head and squinted, considering his options.

I said, "Good. It's settled. You stay here and behave yourself, and then we'll get you home."

Morgan opened the door, and as I got out I kept an eye on Charlie to make sure he stayed put, but he was so pooped he barely moved. The tall redhead was waiting at the curb, and as we joined her, I noticed she was easily a good four inches taller than Morgan. Her skin was pale, threatening to freckle, and she wore a dun-colored blouse with a gray collar, a frayed beige scarf that hung past her waist, and a plain, knee-length skirt that with only a few minor alterations might easily have doubled as a potato sack.

She stepped forward and extended her hand, adjusting the canvas bag that was slung over her shoulder, and just then there came from somewhere inside it the muffled sound of a cell-phone ringing. She ignored it.

I said, "Hi, Detective McKenzie."

She said, "Hi, Dixie."

The first time I met Detective Samantha McKenzie was at the house of one of my former clients, the Harwicks. They lived in a huge, ornate mansion off Jungle Plum Road at the north end of the Key. I'd been hired to take care of their massive tank of exotic fish, as well as their cat, Charlotte, a cantankerous but beautiful Siamese diva with a luxurious, silver-tipped chocolate coat. On my first day there, I found Charlotte lurking around the edge of the swimming pool in the back, tentatively batting one paw at the surface of the water, and when I went out to fetch her I saw a dark shape lying at the bottom of the pool.

That dark shape, unfortunately, turned out to be Charlotte's owner, Mr. Harwick.

Detective McKenzie was assigned to the case—she had just joined the sheriff's office a few months earlier—and the moment she started questioning me, I knew I'd never met anyone like her. The way Detective McKenzie's mind works is unique: it's not unlike a runaway roller coaster. It twists and turns, careening from one track to another at dizzying speeds and with no apparent rhyme or reason. Plus, she's blunt and no-nonsense, which comes off as sheer rudeness. It was only after I'd gotten to know her a little better that I realized it's not rudeness at all, but rather an inability (or flat-out refusal) to adhere to all the social rules and common niceties that the rest of us follow.

To add insult to injury, she also has the unsettling habit of avoiding direct eye contact. Instead, she fixes her gaze just slightly off to the side or at the center of your forehead, which is precisely what she was doing right now.

"I understand you've had quite a shock."

I said, "I'll be fine . . . but the woman inside. Do you know who she is?"

She tilted her head. "I was just about to ask you the same thing."

I said, "No. I have no idea. I couldn't see her face, and everything happened so fast."

Her eyes narrowed, and for a moment I saw a look of confusion flash across her face. "So, you didn't notice . . . ?"

I said, "Didn't notice . . . what?"

A pained smile formed on her lips, which seemed more than anything else to confirm my worst fears. Almost immediately, a trembling started at the base of my spine and crept all the way down to the souls of my feet. If I'd been thinking clearly, I would have turned on my heels right then and headed straight for the Bronco. I figured if I moved fast enough, I could be out the driveway and crashing through those traffic cones before anybody even knew what was happening.

Instead, I took a deep breath.

"Detective McKenzie, didn't notice *what*?"

8

I can't say for certain how long I was standing there, staring at McKenzie's gray eyes and waiting for an answer. It felt like an eternity, but in the time that passed all I managed to do was curl my trembling hands into fists and prop them unsteadily on my hips. The tight smile on McKenzie's face hadn't wavered, but I knew there was something she wasn't telling me. I could see it in her eyes.

She said, "Dixie, I don't mean to alarm you, but I'm afraid I'm going to have to ask you to come inside and take another look."

A voice inside my head murmured, *No way.* There wasn't a snowball's chance in hell I was going back inside that house unless it was to get Franklin and Gigi out. But then I thought of Caroline, and all I could hear was her cheerful voice on the phone . . . *Seriously, Dixie. Is it crazy to get on a boat and go sailing off into the wild blue yonder with a man I barely know?*

I said, "Detective McKenzie, I've had a long day, and

I'm tired, and I need to find a place for Franklin and Gigi to stay for the night, since I'm assuming they can't stay here, and I need to get Charlie home before his owners start worrying. So please, just tell me . . . is it her?"

She frowned. "Is it who?"

I took a deep breath. "Caroline. Is it Caroline's body in there?"

For the first time, her face softened. "Dixie, I'm sorry, but I don't know. I was actually hoping you might be able to answer that."

I took a deep breath. "Sorry. I'm just a little flustered."

"So, you didn't recognize her at all?"

"No. In fact, I thought she was a man at first."

"At first?"

"Yes, because of the suit."

"But then you realized you were wrong when you looked under the scarf."

"No, I didn't look under the scarf."

She nodded. "You overheard Morgan's call to dispatch."

"Yes. He asked me to wait in the car while he checked things out, and I heard everything over the radio."

"So you didn't touch the body at all?"

I frowned. I couldn't tell whether she was trying to figure out if I was stupid enough to tamper with a dead body or if I was stupid enough not to attempt resuscitation.

"I did. I felt the wrist. It was her right arm. She was stiff, and there was no pulse and the skin was stone cold, so I knew right away. And everything happened so fast

I didn't have time to do anything else, and I had Charlie with me. He was still on the porch, so I closed the door and locked it. And then I put Charlie in the car and called 911."

"Why did you lock the house?"

I thought for a moment. "I have no idea. I just did."

"Okay. Let's go have a look, but first . . ."

She stepped aside, and just behind her was the lanky boy I'd seen earlier. He had taken off his red baseball cap and was hugging it to his chest, smiling meekly. I realized he must have been standing there the entire time. I'd been so riled up I hadn't even noticed.

McKenzie said, "Dixie, this is Matthew."

He was dressed in a white oxford button-down a couple sizes too big for his skinny frame, tucked into a pair of faded blue jeans that were practically threadbare at the knees. His mop of white-blond hair was parted neatly to one side, falling across his forehead and shading his eyes. He had a moody, almost sad expression on his face, and before he spoke I would have put his age at somewhere around sixteen and a half.

He put his hand out. "I'm Detective Carthage. Nice to meet you."

His voice was deeper than I had expected, and despite the fact that he seemed rather meek and more than a little awkward, his grip was firm and confident. As I shook his hand, McKenzie absentmindedly adjusted the thin scarf around her neck.

She said, "Yes. *Detective* Matthew Carthage. I promise I'll stop doing that eventually. We're very lucky to have him on our team. He'll be working with me on a few cases, beginning with this one."

I said, "Oh, I thought you were a neighbor . . . or something."

I was about to say *neighborhood kid,* but luckily I stopped myself in time.

He blushed. "I'll be following Detective McKenzie for a few weeks. Learning the ropes, so to speak."

McKenzie reached into her shoulder bag. "Well, now that we've all met each other . . ."

She pulled out an aluminum clipboard with a yellow lined notebook attached, bulging with Post-its and miscellaneous papers folded inside, and as she flipped through the top pages I noticed every square inch from top to bottom was filled with tiny blue handwriting. When she finally came to a blank page, she flipped the whole mess over and secured it to the clipboard with a green rubber band, and then looked me straight in the middle of my forehead.

"Tell me what happened."

At that point, I felt like my brain was swimming in a jar of formaldehyde, but I took a deep breath and did the best I could. I told her everything, starting with my arrival at Caroline's house the day before, and how Charlie had immediately torn through the living room and scratched the parlor door trying to get to the front foyer. I told her how Caroline had gone on a boat trip with her new boyfriend, and how I'd already tried to call her but she hadn't answered, and I told her how I'd fallen asleep on the lounge chair by the pool with Gigi on my lap, and how the woman who lives in the house next door had sent a young man over to find me.

The entire time I was talking she didn't say a word, and even though her pen was poised over her notepad, she didn't write anything either. She just watched and listened, occasionally dropping her chin and tilting her head to the left, as if she were conferring with an imaginary bird on her shoulder, but as soon as I mentioned the young man next door, she stopped me.

"Which house did he come from?"

I pointed at the big mansion next to Caroline's. "This one here. It's . . ."

"Elba Kramer. Yes, I know."

"He said he was her assistant."

Detective Carthage glanced at McKenzie. I imagined he was probably impressed she knew right off the bat who lived next door. He was taking notes on his cell phone, the glow from its screen illuminating his face as his thumbs fluttered over the keyboard with a speed only a teenager could master. His eyes were pale green, his skin clear and smooth, and I wondered whether he was old enough to drive a car, much less be a homicide detective for the Sarasota Sheriff's Department. He'd probably never even heard of Elba Kramer.

If McKenzie noticed his reaction, she didn't let on. "Have you spoken with Ms. Kramer recently?"

I said, "No. I know who she is, of course, but we haven't spoken."

"And yet she knew you were here. Any idea how?"

I shook my head. "I just assumed Caroline must have

mentioned I'd be here taking care of Franklin and Gigi while she was away. Or maybe she saw my car in the driveway."

"And this young man that came over, what did he want?"

"He said Ms. Kramer wanted to know if I took care of birds and if I could come over and meet with her when I was done."

"What did he look like?"

"Short. Boyish face. Dark hair and olive skin, kind of Middle Eastern looking . . . or maybe Indian?"

"And did you?"

"Did I . . . ?"

She sighed impatiently. "Did you go over and talk to her?"

"No. Like I said, I'd fallen asleep. It was late and I needed to get Charlie home, so we made plans to meet tonight. In fact, I need to go over there now and let her know what's happening."

"In fact, no." Without skipping a beat, she turned to Detective Carthage, "Matthew, put somebody on Ms. Kramer's house until I get a chance to speak to her and her husband. If they want to leave, have somebody get me immediately."

He just stood there, staring at his screen with his thumbs paused in midair.

After a moment, McKenzie said, "Right," and then raised one hand like she was hailing a taxi.

Deputy Morgan trotted over. "Ma'am?"

She lowered her chin. "Would you please put somebody on the house next door until I get a chance to speak with them?"

"Yes, ma'am."

"And . . ."

Detective Carthage had gone back to typing on his phone, but without looking up he said, "And if they want to leave, have somebody come get us right away."

Morgan said, "Yes, sir," and crossed the sidewalk to one of the deputies standing at the bottom of the driveway.

McKenzie flipped the pages of her notebook over and closed it. "This assistant, did you get his name?"

I said, "He gave me his card. It's an unusual name . . . Rajinder."

"And do you know if Caroline and Elba Kramer are friendly?"

"No. I mean, Caroline's never mentioned her."

"Alright, then." She dropped her notebook back down in her shoulder bag and then glanced briefly at Detective Carthage. "One more thing before we go in. Other than Caroline and the people next door, does anyone else know you're here?"

I thought for a moment. "Not that I know of. Caroline might have told her boyfriend, but other than that . . ."

"No one? You've not told anyone else?"

"No."

"You told me when you arrived you thought something was wrong."

"Yes."

Her eyes narrowed. "Why is that?"

"Nothing happened in particular, but as soon as I got out of the car, I just had a weird feeling. I didn't really think much of it at the time, but yesterday when I was here, we went in the side door, and Charlie ran straight through the house to the parlor. By the time I got there he had scratched up the door to the front foyer."

She frowned. "Why did you go in the side door?"

"Because . . ."

I'm not sure why I hadn't thought of it before, but now it seemed completely obvious. Everything had happened so fast, and I'd been so worried about Gigi and Franklin and Caroline that I hadn't stopped to put all the pieces together.

I said, "Mr. Scotland!"

She tilted her head to one side. "I'm sorry?"

"There was a man here. I completely forgot. He was on the porch when I drove up yesterday. He was standing on Caroline's porch, and he had a big suitcase. He thought I was somebody else . . . he called me Ingrid."

I had a view of the house across the street just over Detective McKenzie's shoulder, and the entire time I was talking I was staring at its darkened windows. It dawned on me that Mr. Scotland might very well be in there now, watching.

I lowered my voice. "I'm pretty sure he had knocked on Caroline's door, because he told me nobody was home. He said he was here on vacation, I think from Scotland because he had a really strong accent, and I think he had just arrived, but I didn't see a cab or anything. He said he was renting a house here, but he got confused because he lost his glasses at the airport. He showed me the piece of paper where he had the address written down. It said number seventeen. This is number fifteen. So he had the right number, but the wrong house."

Without turning around, McKenzie drew her note-pad back out of her bag. "We're talking about the house across the street, yes?"

I nodded.

"And after he showed you the address, what happened then?"

"We talked for a little bit, but Charlie was barking at him pretty bad. That's why I went in the side door because it's faster and I was trying to get him inside so he wouldn't bark any more."

"And what did this Mr. Scotland look like?"

"Handsome. Tall, with curly hair sprinkled with gray. He had a suit on, white shirt and tie. His shoes were really shiny and black. Clean shaven. Black eyes."

"Did you get his name?

"Rupert. Rupert Wolff."

She clicked the tip of her pen and made a few notes on her notepad while Detective Carthage typed into his phone.

I said, "With two f's. He said the second f was for *friendly*."

Neither of them looked up when I said that, but almost in unison they each raised an eyebrow.

"Oh, and the address was written on a page from a prescription pad, or at least that's what it looked like."

Detective McKenzie said, "And did you notice anything

unusual about this man. Did he seem nervous or upset?"

I thought for a moment and shook my head. "No. The opposite actually."

"How so?"

"He was real smooth, kind of flirty. I got a little creeped out by him, actually."

"Why do you say that?"

"Well, he called me . . . I think his exact words were 'pretty little thing' and he made a comment about my 'booty,' but I snipped that in the bud right away."

"And did you tell this Mr. Scotland your name?"

"I think I did. Why?"

She nodded. "So, you showed him which house was number 17, and then you went inside."

"Yeah."

Her gaze swept across the yard to the front door of Caroline's house, and her eyes grew suddenly vacant.

I said, "What is it?"

She took a deep breath. "It doesn't add up."

"What?"

"Is there anyone upset with you?"

"Upset? With me?"

"Yes. Or anyone you can think of who might have reason to hurt you?"

I shook my head slowly. "No, but . . ."

Detective Carthage looked down at his feet, and just then I felt the hair on the back of my neck stand up. Mc-Kenzie flagged down another deputy.

She said, "As discreetly as possible, let's get somebody on the house across the street." Then she brought her hands together like she was closing a prayer book, and that tight smile reappeared on her lips.

She gestured toward Caroline's front porch.

"Well," she said. "Shall we?"

9

When I was a little girl, I found a baby bird.

Well, to put it more accurately, it found me.

I was in the fifth grade. It was the end of the school year, right before summer break. I'd just gotten out of my last class of the day—Mrs. Bell's Reading and Writing—and I was skipping down the hall minding my own business, making my way with the other kids to the circular driveway where all the school buses were lined up.

When I came out the double doors on the side of the building, I heard the eighth-grade girls' choir practicing in the gymnasium, which doubled as the music room on alternate days after school. It was a separate structure, added some time in the fifties but made of the same sandy limestone blocks as the main building, connected by a long walkway covered with corrugated tin that was painted bright fire-hydrant red.

I knew I had at least another five or ten minutes

before the buses took off, so I dropped my book bag down on the sidewalk and leaned against one of the metal poles to listen. I remember being shocked at how cold the metal felt against my neck, even though it must have been a hundred degrees out, and then something that looked vaguely like a ball of wet dryer lint fell at my feet with a *plop*.

I looked up.

At the top of the pole, where it met the awning over-head, was a metal bracket about two inches wide and six inches long. Tucked into its crook was a tiny bird's nest made of matted twigs and pieces of string. To this day, I can still remember what the choir was singing—"Danny Boy"—and I can still hear their thin voices rising in uni-son as I looked down at the baby sparrow at my feet. It was lying flat on its back and staring up at me with ter-rified eyes . . .

But come ye back when summer's in the meadow
Or when the valley's hushed and white with snow
'Tis I'll be here in sunshine or in shadow
Oh Danny boy, oh Danny boy, I love you so.

I knew right away I'd miss my bus, and I knew when I didn't get off at my regular stop my grandmother would be worried sick, and I knew I'd get in trouble when she found out I'd missed it on purpose. But I also knew I couldn't leave that poor bird alone. It was too young to fly, its feathers were just black downy fluff, and there was no way it could climb back into its nest.

If I'd had a crystal ball, I'd have known right then that Mrs. Bell would eventually come out and help me put him back and that he would in fact survive, but at the time I didn't think there was much hope. The chances his mother would accept him after contact with a human being were slim to nothing. And, even worse, it was entirely possible she'd pushed him out of the nest herself to make room for the stronger chicks. I figured all I'd get for my trouble was a dead sparrow and a broken heart.

I know. It sounds awfully self-centered and morose for a ten-year-old girl, but in my defense, I'd had a bad year. My father had died nine months earlier in the line of duty. He was a fireman, just like my brother is today. He got trapped in a burning building—an old warehouse in downtown Sarasota that turned out to be a storage facility for an illegal cache of fireworks, although no one knew that until it was too late.

Our mom never fully recovered. Even before, it's fair to say she wasn't the most nurturing mother in the world, but our father's death pushed her over the edge. Her drinking grew progressively worse, and not three months later she decided she was due for a little vacation from life, so she packed up a couple of suitcases, drove Michael and me to our grandparents' place, and then disappeared off the face of the earth. I can count on one hand the number of times I've seen her since.

As I knelt down with a sigh and looked into the bird's tiny black eyes, I was naive enough to think I'd already endured enough tragedy in my ten short years to last a lifetime.

I remember thinking, *Why me?*

I was walking along the edge of Caroline's yard with Detective McKenzie and Detective Carthage following close behind, surrounded by flashing emergency lights and strings of police tape, and I'm ashamed to admit those very same words were lurking somewhere in the back of my mind. *Why me?* There'd been a group of deputies talking quietly in the road when we walked over, but now they seemed to have stepped away into the background. In fact, the entire street had grown eerily quiet.

McKenzie said, "Dixie, if you can, try to remember the exact path you took when you arrived, and stay on it."

Caroline's driveway, like most of the houses on her street, isn't poured concrete. It's terra-cotta pavers, set at alternating angles to form a repeating starburst pattern, so as we turned toward the house, I counted the stars at my feet in a vain attempt to keep myself from flying into a panic.

I knew why McKenzie wanted me to follow the same path. She didn't want me disturbing things any more than they already had been. There's a term detectives use, mostly in private, for all the local deputies, police officers, and ambulance drivers that first arrive at a crime scene. It's EMT. Short for "evidence mangling technician." As EMTs move through the scene attending to victims, the likelihood that they'll bring in foreign materials, either from clothing or equipment, is extraordinarily high. It's just as likely they'll take crucial evidence with them when they leave: a microscopic flake of skin stuck to the sole of a shoe or a tiny hair accidentally folded into a hospital sheet.

Every crime is like a puzzle, and the more serious the crime, the greater the number of potential pieces that can be scattered far and wide. In the case of a murder, every single surface—every blade of grass, every stone, every crack in the floorboards—can harbor a crucial secret. It might be a droplet of blood, a piece of dirt lodged in the carpet, or a tiny sliver of foil from a packet of chewing gum. It's all held together as delicately as the winged seeds of a thistle, and just the slightest change in the air can send pieces floating off in every direction, never to be found again. That could mean the difference between solving the mystery of what happened and leaving a murderer to roam the streets.

When we got to the porch steps, I stayed to the right, not necessarily because I remembered how I'd gone before, but because I knew Charlie had been on his leash, and I always keep dogs to the left when I'm walking them. At the big picture window, McKenzie asked me to wait. She went over and stood in the open doorway as she pulled a pair of blue latex gloves out of her bag and slipped them on. There was a camera flash from inside the house.

McKenzie said, "Tom, can we have a minute?"

I heard a man's voice from inside. "Sure, I'm done in here for now anyway."

McKenzie stepped back and the crime scene photographer I'd seen before emerged. There were two cameras hanging from his neck and a small spiral notebook tucked into his breast pocket. He drew McKenzie aside and muttered something under his breath.

She said, "Yeah, let me bag it up first, and then let's get closeup shots of both the front and back."

I glanced up at the Kramer house. It was dark on the third floor, but the curtains in one of the windows had a pale bluish glow, as if lit from within by a television, and just then the curtains parted open and a woman appeared.

She had on a white blouse, or perhaps a nightgown, with a very low-cut opening. It plunged almost to her waist, and even from this distance I could tell its edges were scalloped and embroidered with what looked like lacy flowers. I couldn't quite see her face, but I was pretty sure I recognized her hair immediately. It was long, jet black, and perfectly straight—exactly the way I remembered it when her face had been pasted all over the tabloids and local news shows.

It was Elba Kramer.

I think I must have been in some sort of catatonic state, because the first thing that came to mind was that I might be able to get her attention and let her know I hadn't forgotten our meeting, which of course would have been insane, given the circumstances. Luckily, before I could do anything stupid—like wave or call out her name—the curtains fell back and she disappeared.

The crime scene photographer stepped off the porch and took a couple of pictures of the yard and then moved down the side of the house closest to Ms. Kramer's, taking pictures of just about everything the entire way.

McKenzie turned, her expression somber, and said, "You might want to take a couple of deep breaths."

I didn't follow her advice. My palms were sweaty, and I could feel my heart pounding, but for some reason I wanted her to think I was fine, that I wasn't the fading flower she assumed, that I'd seen a dead body before, and that I couldn't imagine why she suddenly thought I was so delicate.

But I knew it wasn't going to be that simple.

I think I'd been holding on to the possibility that I'd imagined the whole thing, because when I stepped up to the doorway and saw the body again, my heart sank. It was still there, surrounded by blood-soaked magazines and pieces of junk mail, dressed in a man's three-piece suit, light blue, with a green-and-yellow striped tie. There was a black leather belt with a square silver buckle around the waist, and the shoes were black leather too. They seemed newly polished, and I noticed both shoelaces were neatly tied in tight bows.

McKenzie stepped carefully so as not to disturb any of the mail on the floor, and then knelt down next to the body.

She said, "Ready?"

I clenched my fists and nodded. With one gloved hand, she reached out and gently lifted one corner of the scarf.

I gasped.

The girl had short, dark hair. Her face was round and white as snow, with a delicate nose and lips turned a pale shade of lilac. Her mouth was hanging open, as if she'd been interrupted in the middle of an unexpected surprise, and her eyes were fixed on the ceiling. She had a handlebar mustache drawn with what looked like dark brown eyebrow pencil above her lips, and there were long sideburns drawn on either side of her face.

Despite all that, I recognized her right away. "Sara . . ."

McKenzie turned to me, her eyes wide. "What?"

I stammered. "I'm not sure. She looks like someone . . . the girl that works at the food stand at the beach pavilion, but her hair's different. It's blond, almost the exact same color as mine, and she has a pierced eyebrow."

McKenzie leaned in a little closer. At the far edge of the girl's right eyebrow were two tiny, almost imperceptible holes, one above and one just below.

She said, "Do you see that?"

I nodded.

She lifted the scarf a little higher, and now I could see the girl wore a short, dark wig. It had been pulled to one side. Underneath was a stocking cap, covering locks of light blond hair.

I shook my head slowly. "It's her."

McKenzie let the the scarf fall back in place. "I'm thinking perhaps she was on her way to some kind of costume party . . . but there's one more thing."

She lifted the opposite corner of the scarf.

"This . . ."

Peeking out from under the scarf, just above the breast pocket, was a small yellow rectangle about three inches wide and two inches tall. At first, I thought it might have been a business card, but it was folded in half, like one of those placeholders they use at fancy dinners. It was held to the lapel of the jacket with what looked like a hat pin, at least five inches long, at the tip of which was a glistening black pearl, roughly the size of a green pea.

I said, "What is it?"

She motioned me closer. "You tell me."

At the center of the card, written in neat cursive handwriting, were five words . . .

Just then, a strange sensation washed over me. My body felt like rubber, and the ground seemed suddenly unreliable, as if I were standing on a pier that had come unhooked from its mooring and was slowly moving out with the tide.

I whispered, "What does it say?"

But I didn't need her to tell me. I could see it as clear as rain.

It said, *SEE YOU IN HELL, DIXIE.*

10

I woke with a dull throb camped out in the back of my skull, and my lips felt as dry and cracked as a couple of peanut shells. Without even opening my eyes, I knew Ella Fitzgerald was in her favorite position: stretched across my chest with her paws tucked under my chin. Outside, the birds were calling out tentatively to one another, and for a few blissful moments I thought of nothing but the thrum of Ella's soft purrs, mixed with the rhythmic *swoosh* of the waves rolling in on the beach down below.

It had not been a good night.

I hadn't slept well—not a big surprise, considering the circumstances. Every time I came close to falling asleep, a glowing yellow rectangle would float into view, as if it were seared onto the inside of my eyelids, and then I'd watch helplessly as an invisible hand etched a message across the middle of it in delicate curving script, as if hand-lettered with a feathered quill . . .

SEE YOU IN HELL, DIXIE.

Next, Sara Potts's face would materialize, her blue eyes peering over the card, wide and imploring, and then my heart would start racing and I'd bolt up in a sweat. That happened over and over again, to the point where I no longer knew if I was awake or dreaming.

I'd spent the entire night checking the long window that runs along the top of the wall opposite my bed, and now when I opened my eyes, I could just make out the vaguest hint of light beginning to overtake the darkness outside. I ran my hand down Ella's back.

"Finally," I whispered.

Her eyes narrowed to slits. She said, *"Mmmeep."*

Ella got her name from the jazzy scatting noises she makes, and it fits her personality perfectly. She's regal and classy, but with a true rebel's spirit. She's a calico Persian mix, meaning mostly Persian, but her coat has distinct blocks of vivid russet brown, snow white, and charcoal black. She was originally a gift to me from a client that had to leave town unexpectedly, but it didn't take her long to figure out that all the good stuff comes out of Michael and Paco's kitchen. She loves me, I'm sure of that, but her heart belongs to her daddies.

I whispered "sorry" to Ella for disturbing her beauty rest and then rolled over to find Gigi watching me from the bedside table. He'd spent the night in an old hamster cage I found in the attic. I'd laid some rag towels on the bottom to make a soft bed for him, and I'd left a bowl of water and some carrot sticks mixed with a little of Ella's cat kibble in one corner. It wasn't exactly the palatial digs he was used to, but I figured it wouldn't hurt him to see how the other half lives for a night or two until I could take him back home.

He blinked and wiggled his nose, which I took to mean he'd had a better night than I had.

Ella burrowed back under the blankets as I reached out and slipped my fingers through the bars to give Gigi a scratch between his long ears, but he hopped over to the opposite side of the cage. I knew he'd eventually get accustomed to his new surroundings and settle down, but at that point I think he'd had enough human contact for the time being.

I knew exactly how he felt.

I rolled out of bed as quietly as possible and padded into the bathroom, where I pulled my hair back into a ponytail and splashed cold water on my face. I decided I wouldn't tell anybody about what had happened, at least not until after breakfast. For one, I think I was probably in shock. I just wanted to have as nice and normal a morning as possible, and I knew once they found out, I'd get a barrage of questions. But also, Detective McKenzie had explicitly asked me not to talk about the details of the case until she'd had a chance to thoroughly interview everyone involved. So, for now, I decided to put the whole thing out of my mind.

I stared at myself in the mirror and examined my bloodshot eyes.

Easier said than done, I thought.

My poker face is amateur at best. People who know me can usually tell right off the bat if I'm lying or upset, but given the fact that my memory of the night before was already starting to feel like a distant blur, I thought I might get away with it. I'm pretty sure my poor brain was actively trying to block it all out—starting with the moment I laid eyes on that card pinned to Sara Potts's lapel. I remembered Detective McKenzie asking if I knew who might have put it there, and I remembered being afraid I might burst into laughter or tears or both, so I just shook my head . . . *No.*

After that, one of the deputies led me back down the driveway to wait while Detective McKenzie went next door to talk to Elba Kramer. My Bronco had been moved farther down the street, closer to the traffic cones, although I didn't remember giving anybody the key, and then while I was pulling a couple of cardboard cat carriers out of the back, Deputy Morgan told me he'd follow me home—Detective McKenzie didn't want me driving by myself.

Normally, I would have objected. If you haven't figured it out by now, I don't like being treated like a defenseless pansy. But I was too tired to put up a fight. Either that or I'm a defenseless pansy. I just nodded and told him I had to take Charlie home first, and then I called our local cat kennel, the Kitty Haven, to see if they might be able to take Franklin for the night. He couldn't stay at Caroline's, not with the entire place crawling with crime technicians, and I knew Ella wouldn't be too thrilled about a sleepover with a cat she'd never met.

I don't remember going back inside the house at all, but we must have entered through the side portico. Gigi was huddled in the corner of his cage under a cover of hay. I doubted he'd ever had so many strangers walking around his house in his entire life, but once I had him in my arms and cradled in a soft towel, he seemed to calm down.

Franklin was hiding under a row of sundresses in Caroline's walk-in closet. I spotted him right away because his fluffy cream-colored tail was poking out behind a stack of shoe boxes. Luckily, he didn't put up too much of a fight. As we went back through the living room, I saw a couple more camera flashes from the doorway to the front hall, but I didn't look back.

Now, staring at my puffy, sleep-deprived face in the mirror, I dabbed on a little lip gloss and squirted some eyedrops in each eye, though I knew the only real cure was more sleep. After I brushed my teeth and got dressed, I tiptoed back into the bedroom and lifted up one corner of the blanket.

Ella had moved up to the top of the bed and was stretched out full length across my pillow with her head right next to Ethan's. His lips were parted slightly, and Ella's whiskers were brushing against the stubble of his cheek.

Yes . . . Ethan.

The words "yes" and "Ethan" seem to go hand in hand now, but for what seemed like an eternity they'd gone together like oil and water, which isn't saying a thing about Ethan, but it says volumes about me . . .

He is my—for lack of a better word—*boyfriend*. That means a number of things: one, I always know where he is, and for the most part, he always knows where I am. It also means we often spend the night together, always at my place since his apartment looks like it's inhabited by a gang of bachelor pigs (his words, not mine—I've actually never seen it). He runs a one-man law firm, Crane & Sons, which he inherited from his grandfather.

The first time I laid eyes on him, I knew I was in big trouble. He's one quarter Seminole, with high cheekbones and a square jaw, eyes the color of bittersweet chocolate, and lashes so thick they make his eyes look rimmed with kohl. He's a good foot taller than me, with jet-black hair that brushes past his shoulders and a smile that never fails to make me a little weak in the knees.

If all that sounds a little too cliché for your taste, then you understand my problem exactly. In almost every category, he's too good to be true, like a character from a cheap romance novel or a fairy tale. There was a time I believed in fairy tales . . . but I'm not so sure anymore.

Six years ago—six years, one month, and three days to be exact—my husband, Todd, and my daughter, Christy, were both killed in a freak car accident. An old man accidentally ran over them in the parking lot at our local grocery store. Apparently, he thought he had shifted into reverse. He was wrong.

Todd was thirty. Christy was three.

It feels funny to just blurt it out like that, like items on a to-do list or a PowerPoint presentation, but there's really no other way. Sometimes, it seems like it happened on another planet, light-years away, and sometimes it seems like it's happening right now, right here.

At any rate, after Todd and Christy's funeral, I became a blithering idiot. Michael and Paco took care of me the best they could, bringing me food and keeping me relatively clean, but for almost a year I barely got out of bed. My commanding officer at the sheriff's department, Sergeant Woodrow Owens, was probably more patient with me than he should have been, but eventually—and I'll spare you all the ugly details—it became patently clear that I couldn't be trusted to wear a deputy badge, let alone carry a loaded gun around in public. The department asked me to resign, and so I did.

For the longest time, even though I knew he hadn't done it on purpose, I held that old man responsible for taking my family and my life away. I kept him prisoner in a very dark place inside me, my heart like a jail cell. It took a long time before I finally set him free. I don't remember his name. I don't know if he's still alive, and I don't want to know. I'm trying to forgive him.

Todd had been a deputy too. We worked together. We had a good life. We had a little house in Sarasota, not more than fifteen minutes from where I live now, with a nice yard and a little vegetable garden. We'd stagger our shifts so most of the time one of us was home with Christy while the other was at work. We had a babysitter when we needed it, a sweet teenage girl who lived a couple doors down, but I don't remember her name either. In fact, I've blocked out most of my memories from that time. I'm sure they're still bouncing around in my head somewhere, but it's easier not to think about it. And loads better for my sanity as well.

Pet sitting just kind of fell into my lap . . . literally. Michael and Paco had a friend who was looking for someone to take care of her cat while she was out of town. They told her I did a little pet sitting on the side—which of course was a bald-faced lie, but I think they were starting to worry I'd end up in a straitjacket if they didn't come up with something for me to do. It took them a while to talk me into it, but eventually I found myself sitting on the woman's balcony, in a sprawling luxury condo overlooking Sarasota Bay, with a fluffy cat named Rudy sitting in my lap and gazing lovingly into my eyes.

He took care of me for two weeks, and the rest is history.

I like dealing with animals better than humans. For one, a dog might bite your neighbor or dig up your lawn, but he'll follow you to the ends of the earth, no questions asked. And a cat might pee on your pillow, but she'll never betray you.

Ethan stirred in his sleep, and I realized I'd been standing there staring at him for God knows how long, playing through all my old memories like a sappy after-school special. I think seeing that poor girl's lifeless body must have jostled something deep inside me, knocking loose all the ghosts of the things I hold dear and sending them flying out.

I knew Ethan didn't have to be at work for at least another hour, and since Ella's only job is keeping the mice at bay, her schedule is completely flexible. I knelt down next to the bed and gave her a little kiss on the nose, and then I gave Ethan a little kiss on the nose too, and then I tiptoed out and closed the bedroom door softly behind me.

I have to admit—there's something nice about having a man in your bed. It puts a slightly different spin on things. I could even go out on a limb and say: Yes, I like knowing Ethan's there snoozing away on the pillow next to mine. Yes, I like thinking he'll be there when I come home at the end of the day. And, yes, I like pretending I'm not alone in the world.

Is that love?

I don't know.

Let's change the subject . . .

11

In the kitchen, I poured myself a glass of orange juice and leaned against the counter, staring at the off-white coating of the refrigerator door. I could feel my stomach turning into a nervous ball of knots.

It felt more like a dream than a memory—kneeling over that poor girl's body and seeing my name written on that card. How was it even possible? And who could have done such a thing? And why? And the man's suit and the wig and the mustache and sideburns drawn on her face . . . Who even knew I'd be at Caroline's house that day? If the person who'd killed Sara Potts had been the person that left that note, then they must have had information about my schedule. They must have known I'd be arriving at Caroline's house to discover her body . . . but *who*?

I sighed and shook my head slowly. I told myself if there was anyone who could figure it out, it was Detective McKenzie. And then my eyes landed on the little basket at the end of the counter where we keep the mail.

Inside was a single envelope, unopened. It had been there for weeks—an invitation to a wedding. Namely, Guidry's wedding.

Detective Jean Pierre Guidry . . . If you don't recognize that name it doesn't matter, because he's gone now. But to make a long story short—Guidry was the first person who managed to make his way into my heart after it had been dead for so long, after I lost Todd and Christy. Until Guidry, I'd built a thick wall around myself, wrapped in razor ribbon and thorny vines and concrete as thick and impenetrable as the shell of coconut, safely protected from every man, woman, and child. Somehow, Guidry managed to slide through all that like a sharp knife through butter.

He'd been the lead homicide detective for the Sarasota sheriff's department before Samantha McKenzie took over. He was smooth and bronzed, with laugh lines that fanned out from the corner of his kind eyes, a beaky nose, and dark hair cut short, with hints of silver showing at his temples. He taught me that I could feel again, that the heart's table always has room for one more, and that even though Todd and Christy were gone, I owed it to myself and to their memory to keep on living, no matter the consequences.

Of course, that's easier said than done, especially given how bumpy the road of life is. We hadn't been together long when a job offer came in from New Orleans, his hometown. The police department there was looking for a lead detective. It was a good opportunity, and his entire family was there. He would've been crazy to turn it down, so I didn't blame him one bit for accepting. I even considered moving there with him . . . but I couldn't. I couldn't leave Siesta Key and all my memories behind. I grew up here. It's my home.

So, that was that.

I could probably blather on for hours about what Guidry means . . . or *meant* to me . . . but I won't. The last I'd heard from him, he'd called to tell me he was engaged, which was of course confirmed by that wedding invitation. And, by the way, I'm fully aware it sounds like I'm still pining away for him, but I'm not. Truly.

It's just . . . *complicated.*

I opened the refrigerator and peered inside. Behind the orange juice carton was a six-pack of Coronas, and for a split second I considered popping one open, thinking it might clear my mind, but instead I splashed a little more orange juice in my glass and threw open the french doors to the balcony.

Outside, the air was warm and heavy. I welcomed the sensation of it pouring over my body like molten wax. The birds were in full chorus now, the dark sky having morphed into a field of cotton-candy blue, and perched on top of the Bronco was a small brown squirrel, surrounded by empty shells and munching away on an acorn.

"Good morning, sunshine."

Michael was beaming up at me from the deck, dressed in jogging shorts and a tank top, standing next to the big teak table our grandfather built. Laid across it was an off-white tablecloth with an embroidered border of blue cornflowers. In the center were two big bowls: one with fresh mango, pineapple, grapes, blackberries, and kiwi, and the other with heaps of crispy fried bacon.

I nearly burst into tears.

"Oh my God." I took the steps down two at a time like a kid on Christmas morning. "You have no idea how happy I am you're home."

He said, "Oh, please. Don't bullshit me. You're just happy there's bacon."

He turned and started laying forks and knives down on the table as I gave him a bear hug from behind. "Okay, that may be true, but I'm equally happy you're home."

He squeezed my hand. "You and me both."

Michael inherited the same blond hair and fair skin I did, but he's built like a . . . well, like a fireman. He's basically a beefier, hairier version of me, with blue eyes, broad shoulders, and biceps as big around as my thighs. I've heard more than one woman call him a *hunk*, but to me he's just my goofy older brother.

Like our father before us, he works the 24/48 shift at the firehouse, meaning he works two days straight and then has one day off. Most days he cooks for the crew, which can often be as many as a dozen men and women, but Michael loves it. He's always been a provider . . . for as long as I can remember.

I said, "You're up early."

He stretched. "Yeah, I woke up thinking about work yesterday, which totally sucked. I couldn't go back to sleep so I thought I'd go for a jog, but then Paco started making breakfast so I took a shower instead. I didn't think I'd see you until tonight."

"Why's that?"

"Well, you were out pretty late. Paco and I were up reading when you got home last night."

I nodded. "Yeah, I guess it was kind of late."

"But what's Ethan's car doing here?" He glanced over at the carport. "I thought I heard his car leave right after you got home."

I said, "Oh," and then racked my brain for an explanation.

The night before, when I'd pulled in with Deputy Morgan following in his squad car, I had breathed a huge sigh of relief the moment my headlights lit up the carport. Michael's truck was on the left in its usual spot, Paco's Harley was parked next to it, and Ethan's Jeep was right next to my spot.

Of course, I'm always happy when the boys are home, but this was different. It meant I had a whole stableful of big strong men to protect me. Not that I needed it, but I knew if Deputy Morgan thought I'd be spending the night alone, he'd try to convince me to check into a hotel or stay with friends, at least until we figured out why my name had been on that card.

Luckily, he waited just long enough to make sure I got Gigi safely up the stairs and inside, and then he turned around and drove back down the lane toward the main road.

I said, "Oh. That was nobody."

"Nobody?"

"Yeah, or a tourist. They saw me turn in and followed me up to the house. I think they thought it was an access road to the beach or something."

"That's weird."

I shrugged, trying to change the subject. "It's that time of year. Just yesterday morning a couple pulled up in a big SUV and walked all over the property."

"Lost tourists?"

"That's what I thought at first, but no. They were searching for property to build on. And they looked like they could practically afford to buy the whole island."

Just then Paco emerged from the main house, balancing a platter of sand-dollar-size pancakes in one hand and a coffee carafe in the other. His hair was tousled and he was still in his pajamas: a white tank top and cotton pants printed all over with little cowboys. As he shuffled by, he gave me a kiss on the cheek.

He said, "Hi, sexy."

Where Michael is fair and muscled, Paco is slim, dark, and handsome, with olive skin and a regal profile, not unlike a prince right out of the pages of *The Arabian Nights*. He's an agent for Sarasota's Special Investigative Bureau. He and Michael have been together so long—almost fifteen years now—that he feels like family.

Paco circled around Michael and put the pancakes and coffee down on the table.

Michael said, "Hey, don't I get a kiss too?"

Paco rearranged the silverware on the table. "Nope."

"Why?"

"You're in trouble."

"Huh? What did I do?"

He straightened up and leveled Michael with his dark brown eyes. "Well, who made breakfast?"

"Um. You."

Paco nodded. "That's right. And when I make break-fast, what are you supposed to do?"

"Um, take a shower?"

Paco rolled his eyes. "No. Guess again."

Michael said, "Um, sit around and look handsome?"

"Very funny. You're supposed to get the paper."

Michael grimaced. "Oh, yeah. I forgot."

I said, "I'll get it."

Paco said, "No, you sit down. I'll get it." He rolled his eyes at Michael again and set off down the lane.

Michael loaded up a plate and handed it to me. "Must have been a good party last night. You look beat."

"It wasn't a party. One of my clients had a . . . a thing they had to go to, so they asked me to stay late is all."

I drizzled a little syrup on my pancakes, conscious of Michael's eyes on me. The older he gets, the more I see our father in him, which of course is sweet on the one hand and annoying as hell on the other, but I can't exactly blame him. Our grandparents gave us the happiest and safest childhood anyone could ever hope for, but Michael has felt responsible for me ever since we were little kids. In all honesty, I'm grateful, but sometimes it makes me feel like a perennial teenager.

Michael said, "We had a big fire down on Turtle Bay. Some fool fell asleep on his boat with a kerosene lamp and kicked it over."

I winced. I hate knowing the details of Michael's job. Picturing him running around in a fire makes my stomach hurt.

"That's terrible. Is he okay?"

"Yeah. Smoke inhalation, but he managed to make it

to the dock before it got out of control, so he's fine . . . can't say the same thing for his boat, though. Or the two boats he was moored next to. One of them sank and the other looks like a big floating hunk of charcoal now."

I shook my head. "Ugh. I can't stand thinking about it. Let's talk about something else."

Paco came back up the driveway with the paper tucked under his arm and a distant look on his face. He sat down in silence opposite me and unfolded the paper.

Michael stifled a grin. "So, how was your walk?"

"Fine." He turned the page without looking up. "The magnolia tree is blooming."

Michael said, "Nice."

"And it looks like we've got a family of rabbits living at the base of it."

"Oh, that's cool."

Paco nodded. "Mm-hmm. I've got some carrot tops I might take down there after breakfast." He turned the page again. "Oh, and there's a sheriff's deputy staked out at the top of the driveway."

Michael's jaw dropped open. "A *what*?"

"A sheriff's deputy. Dixie, any idea what he's doing there?"

He lowered the paper so I could see his eyes.

I said, "Huh?"

12

I always tell people I've never been across the Florida state line, but it's a lie.

My mother took us on a surprise out-of-state trip when I was six years old and Michael was only eight. It was Christmas season, our father was working the overnight shift at the firehouse, and she had woken us up just as the sun was rising. Her face was flushed and there was a giggling exuberance about her that meant she'd already been drinking, either that or she'd been up all night and had never stopped. While she stuffed some of our clothes into a suitcase, she told us we were going on a "secret adventure," which we both instinctively knew meant our dad didn't know a thing about it.

The real adventure began about thirteen hours later, when she sobered up and found herself stranded on a train platform in a little town in Georgia, with two hungry, exhausted kids in tow and not a single quarter to call home. I remember rummaging through her purse because she couldn't find her sunglasses, and I remember being afraid to ask why she needed them since the sun had long gone down. I finally found them in one of the interior pockets, hiding under a collection of little glass bottles and a crumpled receipt from Maas Brothers department store.

I can still see them. They were the big round kind with dark lenses—the ones you see on trendy models in vintage magazines from the sixties—with a tortoiseshell frame and two parallel rows of sparkling rhinestones arching across the top. As I handed them up to her, I noticed her eyes were bloodshot and glassy.

It was at that point that Michael took control. He marched over to a Salvation Army Santa that was standing just outside the ticket office and, with his eight-year-old face set in solemn, grave lines, said, "My little sister and I need help. Our mother is sick and we have to take her home."

I think right then, at that exact moment, Michael came to the realization that his childhood had ended, that when our father wasn't around to make sure we were safe, he was in charge. It was also the moment I knew that I could always depend on him.

Today, there are a growing number of silver hairs sprinkled throughout his blond locks, and I'm sorry to report that I'm probably responsible for most if not all of them. He inherited our father's quiet stoicism, but he also got a good dose of our mother's nervous anxiety, so whenever there's even the tiniest bit of trouble, he takes it hard. The entire time I was talking, he kept his face buried in his hands, propped up on the table with his elbows.

I recounted the whole sordid story, beginning with my arrival at Caroline's house two days earlier, how Mr. Scotland had been on Caroline's porch with his big suitcase, and how Charlie had raced through the house and scratched up the living room door trying to get to the front foyer. I told them how after I'd cleaned Gigi's cage, we'd all gone out to the lanai and fallen asleep on one of the lounge chairs, and how the young man from next door had woken us up.

Paco's disposition is calm and quiet, the opposite of Michael's, so he's better at keeping his cards close. Until then he'd sat quietly and listened, but now he interrupted me.

"He broke into the house?"

"No, no, no. Nothing like that. He works for the woman next door. She has a bird—a reticulated yellow something or other. I was supposed to meet with her after I stopped at Caroline's but . . . that never happened."

Paco said, "Wait a minute. Are we talking about who I think we're talking about?"

Michael said, "Who?"

Paco's eyes narrowed. "Elba Kramer?"

I nodded.

Michael said, "*The* Elba Kramer?"

"Yep. The very one. She lives next door."

Paco said, "I thought so. She and her husband run a shop downtown—jewelry and perfume and stuff—and she always has her bird with her. She treats it like her own child."

Michael frowned. "Since when are you hanging around in jewelry shops?"

Paco ignored him. "It seems like trouble follows that woman around like a shadow. Did you meet her yet?"

I shook my head solemnly. "No. I never got the chance."

"Why?"

"Because when I opened Caroline's front door, there was a woman lying on her back in the middle of the front hall."

Paco frowned. "Huh?"

"Yeah. At first I thought it was a man. She had a suit and tie on, with a scarf over her face."

"What was she doing there?"

"Nothing." I paused for a moment. "She was dead."

Paco's fork fell to the table and Michael's eyes widened with alarm.

I nodded solemnly. "I knew right away. And I could tell she'd been there for a while. She was stone cold."

Michael said, "Wait. Are you sure?"

Paco glanced at Michael and then back at me.

I said, "Am I *sure* . . . ?"

Michael shook his head. "Sorry. Stupid question."

Paco laid his hand on Michael's back and patted him softly. He said, "Okay, the important thing is Dixie's fine, right?"

At that point, I could have told them how I went sneaking around outside Caroline's house and nearly got blown away at close range by Deputy Morgan, but I was pretty sure that kind of detail might send Michael into a full-on freak-out. I said, "I'm fine. A little frazzled around the edges, but fine."

Paco said, "Was she a friend of Caroline's?"

"I don't know. Caroline's on a boat somewhere with

her new boyfriend and she's not answering her phone. But one thing I know for sure: she would have told me if anybody else was going to be in that house while she was away."

"And when is she coming back?"

"She said she'd be gone about a week and that she'd let me know."

Michael said, "So . . . you have no idea who this girl is?"

I sighed. "After the police got there, the detective took me back inside the house to see if I could identify her. I recognized her right away. She works at the snack bar down at the pavilion on Siesta Beach. Her name is Sara."

Paco closed his eyes and shook his head slowly. "Yeah. I know her."

Michael said, "Wait, the blond girl? The one with the pierced eyebrow?"

"That's her. Sara Potts. Except she was wearing a wig. And she had a mustache and sideburns drawn on her face with a black makeup pencil."

They both just stared at me, speechless. I could tell Michael was still searching my expression for something that might indicate I was making the whole thing up, but I just shook my head.

Paco said, "How was she killed?"

"I don't know. I'm not sure anybody does, or if they do they didn't tell me. They're probably waiting for the coroner's report, but . . . there was blood on the floor around her."

Paco sat back in his chair and folded his arms over his chest. "Wow."

"I know."

Michael's voice was soft. "She was such a sweet girl. I mean, we just talked to her like a month ago." He turned to Paco. "Remember? We saw her on the beach at the sand-sculpture contest. She was about to start grad school at Florida State. She was all excited about it."

I laid my head down on the table with a sigh.

Michael was right, she *was* a sweet girl, and always ready with a smile for everybody. I couldn't even count the number of times she'd waited on me at the snack bar, always more cheerful than any of the other kids that worked there, offering free soda refills and piling the french fry baskets to overflowing. Such trivial things, but they said a lot about the kind of person she was.

I looked up at Paco, noting how quiet he'd gotten, and felt a lump form at the base of my throat. Paco is smart . . . like, *scary* smart. He can usually read me like a book, and I could tell he was beginning to suspect I was leaving something out. Meanwhile, Michael looked like he was launching into full denial mode. I knew he was already hoping we'd change the subject.

After a few moments, Paco said, "So, anything else? Do they know how she got in the house?"

"Not yet. It was locked when I got there, so unless she had a key, or somebody locked it after . . ."

Paco fixed me with his dark brown eyes. "I still don't quite understand. Why do we have a sheriff's deputy guarding the house?"

"Well . . . there is one more thing . . ."

Michael closed his eyes and tilted his head back. "Please make it stop."

I said, "It's not that big a deal. Well, okay, it's pretty weird, but I don't want you guys to get all upset about it."

Michael's eyes widened. "You mean, weirder than a dead woman in a wig and a man's suit with a mustache and sideburns painted on her face?"

I gulped. "Maybe. I'm only telling you because you should probably know . . . just in case . . . but you can't tell a soul. Detective McKenzie doesn't want any of the details getting out before she's had time to thoroughly investigate the whole thing."

Michael groaned. "Then don't tell us."

Paco said, "What is it?"

I took a deep breath. "There was a card, like a calling card. It was pinned to her lapel. And the thing is . . . my name was on it."

Paco frowned. "What do you mean?"

"It said, 'See you in hell, Dixie.'"

I don't know what I was expecting their reaction would be. At the very least, I thought Michael might jump up from the table or Paco would laugh, assuming I was playing some kind of sick practical joke on them, but they both just sat there in stunned silence. Finally, Michael reached over, picked up Paco's fork, and let it fall to the table again with a clatter.

Paco said, "So, that explains our friend in the driveway."

Just then, Ethan appeared on the balcony with Ella cradled in his arms, both of them sleepy-eyed and blinking in the sunlight. Ethan had a slightly puzzled look on his face, which made sense given he'd been sound asleep when I got home the night before and I hadn't woken him up.

He said, "Umm, there's a rabbit on the nightstand."

I nodded. "Yeah."

"I mean, like . . . a real, live rabbit."

I motioned him to join us. "Yeah, I know. And there's more. Come eat and I'll explain everything."

He hesitated, glancing first at Paco and then at Michael.

Michael closed his eyes. He was drawing slow circles on his temples with the tips of his index fingers.

He said, "If I were you, I'd go back to bed."

As I drove away from the house, with the wild parakeets chirping and twittering in the treetops, I prepared myself for the worst. If history was any indication, I knew the moment I saw Deputy Morgan staked out at the top of the driveway, everything that had happened in the past twenty-four hours would suddenly become real and I'd dissolve into a panicked mess . . . but I was wrong.

Morgan's car was parked on the side of the road, facing north and completely blocking the entrance. His deputy hat was pulled down low on his forehead, his eyes hidden behind silver-mirrored sunglasses. When he heard my approach, he gave a quick, somewhat apologetic wave and then backed out of the way. I saw him clear a collection of paper coffee cups off the front dash as I rolled by, and then when I turned toward the center of town, he pulled in behind and followed at a discreet distance.

To my utter surprise, I wasn't a mess. In fact, I didn't feel the slightest bit upset. More than anything, I was *annoyed*.

What a giant, colossal waste of department resources.

The fact that McKenzie had tagged me with a twenty-four-hour surveillance detail felt like a joke. Or, better yet, a slap in the face. Just because I was a material witness to a crime, she'd decided a uniformed doofus with a shiny brass badge on his chest was the answer to all my problems, as if I couldn't possibly take care of myself. As if the existence of my name on that card meant I was in some kind of immediate mortal danger. As if there was some kind of homicidal lunatic with a grotesque sense of humor, roaming the streets and waiting to pounce on me.

I rolled my eyes and shook my head again, this time with an added sarcastic chuckle.

"As if . . ."

13

Ethan had taken the news of our overnight security guard surprisingly well. I had expected him to be at least as dramatic as Michael had been, but I think he must have considered what it would have done to me if he'd shown more than cautious concern about it. Instead, he told me not to worry, that obviously the sheriff's office was just doing their job—covering all their bases and so forth—and that he was 100-percent certain Detective McKenzie would soon have a logical explanation for everything that had happened.

He also canceled his appointments for the day and told me he'd work from home, "just in case."

I didn't argue. Especially since it meant he could babysit Gigi.

"Custom House. How may I help you?"

I was pulled over to the side of the road just past Sea Plume Way, and Deputy Morgan was idling in his cruiser about a hundred feet behind me. I squinted my eyes, trying to read the fine print on the calling card that

Elba Kramer's assistant had given me, but it wasn't easy. My sunglasses were all smudged and covered in several years' worth of scratches from rattling around in the glove compartment. I pulled them off and tossed them in the backseat.

I said, "I think I must have the wrong number. I was trying to reach Ms. Kramer . . . ?"

"I am Rajinder, the house manager. Who may I say is calling please?"

"Oh. This is Dixie Hemingway. We met at Caroline's house next door, I was supposed to—"

"Ah, yes. And how is Charlie?"

"Oh, Charlie's fine. His folks are back home now, so I'm all on my own today."

There was a short pause, and then he said, "That's good news. Ms. Kramer has been eager to hear from you. Please hold."

I glanced up in the rearview mirror. Morgan's chin had dropped to his chest, so all I could see was the top of his deputy hat floating behind the steering wheel. I wondered if he'd gotten any more sleep than I had.

"This is Elba Kramer."

She spoke in a smoky half-whisper, as thick as syrup but tinged with color, like the brassy high notes of a saxophone, mixed with just the slightest hint of a southern accent—exactly as I'd imagined the Scarlet Woman of Siesta Key would sound.

I said, "Oh, hi Ms. Kramer, this is Dixie Hemingway. We were scheduled to meet last night . . . ?"

"I know. When I heard you scream, I called the police immediately. I didn't realize they were already there until I saw everyone walking around. What a terrible, terrible thing! I can hardly believe it. I hope you're okay?"

"I'm fine. I was just calling to explain why I never showed up, but I guess you already figured that out."

She said, "No need to apologize. The detective told me everything. Oh, that poor girl. Did you know her? It must have been quite a shock. I can't even imagine. After I talked to that detective, not the guy in the suit, but the other one—I forget her name. Very strange woman . . ."

I said, "That's Detective McKenzie."

"Yes. McKenzie. After she was done questioning me, I told her I'd come outside to find you. But she said it was a bad idea, and by that time all the reporters were hovering about, and . . . well, I don't like reporters very much."

For a split second, a series of images flashed in my mind like still frames from a movie montage: me, headed for the limo outside Todd and Christy's funeral, surrounded by TV crews, a reporter sticking her microphone in my face: *How does it feel to lose a husband and child in such a senseless way?* My mouth twisting in rage as I lunged for her, wanting nothing less than to rip her from limb to limb, and then Michael and Paco pulling me off and holding me in a bear hug, as tight as a straitjacket . . .

I said, "Well, Ms. Kramer, I don't blame you. I don't much care for reporters either."

She said, "Oh, honey, I think we're gonna get along splendidly."

Tell her, I heard a voice in my head say.

It seemed unnecessary, but still I wondered if I wasn't

being dishonest—not telling her our paths had crossed before. But, then again, I wondered if maybe she already knew and didn't care. Maybe it would just be embarrassing to bring up the whole affair on the boat with Senator Cobb after all these years.

I could hear what sounded like the tinkling of ice being dropped in a glass in the background. She said, "Could you be here the day after tomorrow at five thirty? I realize with everything that's happened you're probably in shock . . ."

I said, "No. That's totally fine, but I did have one question: Have you by any chance heard from Caroline?"

There was a short pause. "No, honey. And I don't think I will."

I said, "Oh."

I heard a small laugh. "Miss Hemingway, I guess no one's told you, but Caroline and me, we're not exactly friends."

I felt as if I'd walked right into a patch of quicksand. "Oh, gosh, I'm sorry. I just haven't been able to get ahold of her, so I thought maybe . . ."

"Oh, please. How could you know? To be honest, I haven't spoken to Caroline in years. Like most stories in which I'm involved, it's a long and sordid one. When we're best friends, I'll tell you all about it."

People tend to blurt out their deepest, darkest secrets to me, even perfect strangers, so I didn't doubt her one bit. Just one week earlier, I'd been in line at the grocery store and picked up one of those gossip magazines off the rack to pass the time. The headline read: ANGELINA

DEVASTATED! MY HUSBAND IS A LIAR! Underneath was a blurred picture, like a freeze-frame from a television show or a movie still, with Angelina Jolie looking distraught and close to tears.

As I put the paper back, the elderly woman in line behind me leaned over and whispered, "My husband's been lying to me for thirty years. I'd cut his pecker off if I thought I could get away with it!"

I didn't know what else to say, so I just tightened my lips into a smile and pushed my basket in a little closer to the checkout girl for good measure.

Elba had pulled the phone away from her ear and was cooing at her assistant. "Oh, grapefruit! Raji, how lovely. Take it out to the pool, I'll be right there." A high-pitched chirp sounded in the background. "That's Jane. She says hello."

I said, "Oh, Jane's your bird?"

"Calamity Jane! Raji tells me you have experience with birds?"

"I do. One of my clients has an African grey parrot named Big Bubba that I've taken care of for years."

"Wonderful. You'll love Jane. She's the most fabulous little thing—I never go anywhere without her. She's the light of my life! Five thirty, then? It's important you're not late . . ."

I said, "Not a problem. I'm always on time."

I rang off and glanced in the rearview mirror, half hoping Morgan wouldn't be there, but of course he was.

I whispered, "Well, it's worth a try."

As soon as I got out of the car, he rolled down his

window. I got the impression he was already suspecting I might try to get rid of him, but then he took off his sunglasses.

It wasn't Morgan.

I didn't recognize him at all. He rose out of the car, big and burly, with broad rolling shoulders and a slight paunch—the imposing body of a man who enjoys his food. There was a patch of orange freckles across his pudgy cheeks, and as he tipped his hat I saw a glint of curly copper hair peeking out from underneath. I guessed his age at about twenty-five. A rookie.

Like putty in my hands, I thought to myself.

I said, "Hi. I'm Dixie."

He tipped his hat again. "Yes, ma'am. I know."

"Is this really necessary?"

He looked around. "What?"

"All this." I drew a circle in the air with his face in the center. "I know you're just doing your job, but having an armed escort follow me around all day isn't exactly good for business. I don't want my clients thinking I'm some kind of criminal. And anyway, you probably don't know this, but I'm an ex-deputy myself."

He slipped his sunglasses back on. "I'm sorry, ma'am. I was asked to follow you."

"By who?"

"Sergeant Woodrow Owens."

I nodded curtly and said, "Mm-hmm."

Sergeant Owens had been my direct superior when I was on the force. It was Owens that had called me into the station, just a few weeks after Todd and Christy were killed. It was Owens who told me I was unfit, both emotionally and physically, for further duty, and it was Owens who had accepted my badge and firearm when I handed them over. I had tremendous respect for him then, and I still do. Plus—and I'm woman enough to admit it—I'm just a *teensy* bit scared of him.

I said, "Mm-hmm," again and then started to head back to the car but stopped. "And what's your name again?"

"Hank. Hank Marshall."

I dropped my chin and glared at him. "Seriously?"

"Yes, ma'am. Is there a problem?"

I said, "So . . . your name is Deputy Marshall?"

He shrugged. "That's me."

"Alright, then." I turned and headed back for the Bronco, waving my hand in Deputy Marshall's general direction like I was tossing a trail of breadcrumbs behind me. "Carry on."

I may look like a dumb blonde, and I'll gladly admit I sometimes act like one too, but it comes in handy on occasion. In this particular instance, for example, I commended my brain for the remarkable job it had done so far ignoring the reality of the situation I was in. But now, as I made my way up Midnight Pass to my first client with an armed guard watching my every move, I couldn't ignore it any longer . . .

This was serious.

When McKenzie had asked if there was anyone who might wish me harm, I'd immediately said I couldn't think of a single soul, but we both knew it wasn't true. There were probably hundreds. As a deputy with the Sarasota Sheriff's Department, I'd conducted an untold number of arrests, I'd issued hundreds of tickets for reckless behavior and DUIs, I'd testified against all kinds of burglars and drug dealers, I'd hunted down deadbeat dads, hit-and-run drivers, juvenile delinquents, scam artists, wife beaters, husband beaters . . . There was no telling how many people might wish me ill, out of revenge, a perverted idea of justice, or just plain evil.

I shook my head to clear it, but all that did was send my thoughts flying around like tiny plastic flakes in a snow globe, so I tried my old standby for calming frazzled nerves: I counted birds.

Our little island is only a mile wide and not more than six or seven miles long, but despite that there are about fifty miles of winding canals and waterways within its borders. That means we've got a whole lot of water, countless ponds and lagoons, all lush and fertile as the garden of Eden. From above, it looks like a giant green-and-blue jigsaw puzzle. If you hired a team of crack wildlife experts to design the perfect bird habitat, they'd probably come up with something very close to what we call home.

There's just about every kind of bird you can think of: gulls, terns, white herons, brown pelicans, black-necked stilts, double-breasted cormorants, spoonbills, storks, cranes—and those are just the ones that hang out shoreside. Then there are the cuckoos, the owls, the warblers, the finches, the swallows . . . the list literally goes on and on.

I spotted a couple of morning doves perched on top of the traffic light at the corner of Midnight Pass and Stickney Point, and then beyond that was a flock of swallows swooping over the treetops. A little farther up, wading around in the shallow fountain in front of the Beachhead condo building, was a snowy egret, her feathered crown like a fright wig perched on top of her skinny head.

Just then, I caught my reflection in the rearview mirror and raised one eyebrow.

"And then there's you," I muttered out loud . . .

"A *sitting duck.*"

14

Ninety-nine percent of my days start out at Tom Hale's condo. Tom's an accountant and works from home, but he uses a wheelchair, so I go over twice a day—first thing in the morning and then again in the afternoon—to run with his retired racing greyhound, Billy Elliot. In exchange, Tom deals with my taxes and anything else having to do with money, which is good because I can't balance a checkbook to save my life.

Billy and I usually do a few laps around the circular parking lot that surrounds the building, and then if there's nobody else around, I let him off the leash so he can do a few more laps at a respectable pace. He's not near as quick as he used to be (who is?), but when we're riding back up in the elevator, both of us panting and grinning ear to ear, I know he couldn't care less. He just likes to get out there and relive his glory days. I actually hate running, but I'd be a hot mess if it weren't for Billy Elliot. He's like my own personal trainer.

Deputy Morgan had spent another night staked out at the top of our driveway, but at some point before I left for the day, Deputy Marshall had taken his place again. I waved to him as I came out of the Sea Breeze's lobby. He was sitting in his cruiser, parked by the curb just opposite mine. I heard his engine start up as soon as I headed across the parking lot, but when I opened the car door, something caught my eye. It was small and yellow, stuck down in the cushion behind the seat. I'd left my windows open the night before, so at first I thought it was just a leaf that had floated in, but I was wrong. It was a piece of paper from a pocket-size notebook, with words neatly written in bold, felt-tip pen . . .

Dear Current Owners,

My wife and I would very much like to talk to you about your house. Would you consider selling?

We are quite interested, and are prepared to make a convincing offer.

We're here for a few more days. Please call our mobile.

Yours,

Garth and Edith Reed

Underneath the signature was a telephone number with an area code I didn't recognize, but I figured it was probably from a big northern city, like New York or Chicago.

I don't know why I hadn't noticed the note before, except that I'd probably been sitting on it ever since Mr. and Mrs. Got-Rocks paid me a surprise visit that morning. "Current owners," I muttered under my breath. "The *gall* of some people."

I remembered the man had disappeared under the carport for a few moments. He must have left the note on the front seat then, at any rate, I had no intention of calling, no matter how "convincing" their offer. I folded the note and slipped it down in my back pocket, giving Deputy Marshall a thumbs-up as I climbed in behind the wheel. He replied with a short nod, and then followed me all the way around the circular driveway and out the main road.

My last stop of the morning was the Wincocks, a couple I'd only spoken to on the phone so far. I didn't know much about them, other than that Daphne Wincock was an art professor at Florida State University, and her husband, Jackson, was a retired assistant district attorney for Sarasota County. They were catching a flight out of town the next day.

I turned down Sandy Crane Street, just north of the center of town, and kept an eye out for number 27. Mrs. Wincock had told me I couldn't miss it, and she was right. Just like all its neighbors, the house was small—probably not much more than a thousand square feet—but what it lacked in size, it made up in personality. The house was robin's egg blue, with striped pink-and-white awnings over all the windows and a wide pebbled walkway leading to the front porch, lined on either side with devil's-tongue cacti, marigolds, and Mexican sunflowers. On the wall next to the door was a hand-carved wooden plaque that read GUARD CAT ON

DUTY—HISS OFF! And there was a white rectangular rug in front of the door with blue lettering and a blue border, like the name tags they hand out at PTA meetings and hotel conferences. It read, HI, MY NAME IS MAT.

Before I could knock, the door opened to reveal a tanned woman in her midsixties, with a kind face and curly salt-and-pepper hair. Her dark brown eyes were magnified behind cat's-eye glasses, and she had a slightly bemused, slightly chagrined expression on her face.

I said, "Hi, I'm Dixie Hemingway, the cat sitter."

She nodded. "Well, Dixie Hemingway, the cat sitter, you're about to get a quick education on what it's like to live with a madman. Come on in."

She led me into a brightly lit living room, where a man with a bushy mustache and painter's coveralls was on his hands and knees in the middle of a large cotton tarp, completely surrounded by small piles of dowels and knobs, along with what looked like about a hundred little wooden hammers.

Mrs. Wincock said, "Dixie, this is my husband, Jackson."

He stood up and said, "Welcome to *her* nightmare!"

He had a smile as wide as a ten-gallon hat, with a Texas accent to match, and everything he said seemed to end with an exclamation point and a wink.

"Jackson Wincock. Nice to meet ya!" He shook my hand firmly. "That's not my porn name, by the way. It's the one my mama put on the sales receipt!"

Mrs. Wincock shook her head at me. "I warned you."

There was a twinkle in the man's eye that made me

like him immediately. His face was carved with laugh lines, and I guessed he was older than Mrs. Wincock by at least a decade. Where she was neat and trim and reserved, Mr. Wincock was round-bellied and booming, like a bar extra in a John Wayne movie.

He said, "Did you have any trouble finding us?"

"No, sir," I said. "I know the Key like the back of my hand."

He grinned. "I guess that means you're one of them rarified full-time residents."

I nodded. "Yep. In fact, I still live in the house I grew up in, down Midnight Pass Road, right by Turtle Beach."

He said, "Well, I hope you'll pardon the mess, Miss Dixie, but I'm smack dab in the middle of a project here."

Mrs. Wincock raised one eyebrow. "The *middle*?"

He tilted his head from side to side like a metronome. "Well, not the *very* middle exactly, but definitely somewhere past the beginning, and yet not quite at the end. I'll be done in no time, darlin', don't you worry!"

She rolled her eyes. "He's been telling me that for years."

I looked around at all the various piles. "What . . . what are you doing?"

"It's a harpsichord!" He pointed to two big harp-shaped pieces of wood leaning in the corner of the living room. "That's the main body, and then these are all the little doohickeys that go inside it, in one order or another."

I said, "Wow, that's impressive. I don't think I've ever met anyone who built their own harpsichord."

Mrs. Wincock said, "And you still haven't."

I said, "Are you a musician?"

They looked at each other and then turned to me in unison, "No."

"He's a kook is what he is."

Mrs. Wincock hooked her arm around mine and led me through the living room into the kitchen, where there was a wide bay window overlooking a tidy, manicured garden. Perched on top of a yoga pillow in the middle of the deep window sill was a pure-white Turkish Angora.

I said, "Oh, my gosh. What a beautiful cat! What's her name?"

Mrs. Wincock smiled. "Meredith Heedles. We call her Maddy for short, but she prefers Mrs. Heedles. She owns the place. We just live here."

At the sound of her name, the cat looked in our direction. Her eyes were a beautiful beryl green. She appraised me up and down and then turned back to the window. Outside, there were two teak benches along a bamboo fence at the far end, nestled among pots of herbs and blooming camellias, and in the middle was a wall of carefully stacked river stones, with a stream of water spilling over the top and tumbling down into a lily pond about the size of a kiddie pool.

Mrs. Wincock cooed. "Sweetheart, Dixie's going to take care of you while we're away for a couple of days."

I held out my hand. "Hi, Mrs. Heedles."

She sniffed the air tentatively and then raised herself up, pressing into my fingers as she ran her sides along the back of my hand. Her fur was thick and luxurious, and I was thinking it was probably about the softest thing I've ever felt in my life.

I said, "Oh, Mrs. Wincock, before I forget, I'll need your vet's number, and I'll need some contact information while you're away."

Mrs. Wincock pushed her cat's-eye glasses a little farther up the bridge of her nose and glanced back into the living room. Mr. Wincock had switched the TV on, and I could hear the theme music from our local newscast playing in the background. She said, "Oh, you can just use the number I gave you. That's my cell phone."

I pulled out my notebook. "I know, but if you don't mind, I've learned the hard way that it's good to have at least one additional contact number, like the name of your hotel, maybe?"

Her cheeks flushed as she glanced around the room. "Oh. I've got it written down here somewhere. It's called the, uh . . . Hotel Orleans."

"As in . . . *New* Orleans?"

She suddenly looked like a kid caught with her hand in the cookie jar. "Yes."

I hesitated. "Oh, I know someone who lives there, he used to live here but . . ." My voice trailed away as Mrs. Wincock slowly removed her glasses.

She said, "I know, dear. It was Jean Pierre Guidry who told us about you."

"Oh."

"Before my husband retired, he and Guidry worked on a lot of cases together. We're old friends."

I could feel all the muscles in my face tightening into stone as I tried to force my mouth into a polite smile.

She said, "I'm sorry, Dixie. I should have told you when we spoke on the phone. I know all about how you and Guidry used to be . . ."

I said, "Oh, please, don't be ridiculous. It's completely fine. Guidry and I are just friends now. Are you going to New Orleans for business or pleasure?"

She frowned. "Well . . . we're going to the wedding."

"You mean, the *wedding* wedding?"

"Yes, it's this week."

I could feel my cheeks turning hot. "Oh, my gosh. I feel like a complete idiot. I didn't realize it was already . . . I mean, I got the invitation and everything, but things have been so crazy. He's probably wondering why I never responded."

The expression on her face spoke volumes. I cast my eyes around the room, doing my best to look as breezy and carefree as possible. "So, will it be a big wedding?"

Mrs. Wincock slipped her glasses back on. "Well, you know Guidry. He doesn't have a lot of friends. Always busy with work. But Monica comes from a big family, so . . ."

"Monica?"

". . . that's his fiancée."

I nodded enthusiastically. "Oh, right," I said. "I totally forgot."

She smiled warmly. "I don't blame you one bit. Let me show you the rest of the house."

After the tour, I gave Mrs. Heedles a good scratch between the ears and told her it was a pleasure meeting her, and then we went back through the living room, where Mr. Wincock was back on his hands and knees, tinkering with his harpsichord project. The TV was still on, and there was an earnest-looking woman gazing intently into the camera, jabbering away in front of a mobile news van with a big satellite dish perched on top. I remember telling Mr. Wincock that Mrs. Heedles would be in very good hands while they were in New Orleans, at which point he shot Mrs. Wincock a bewildered look, but neither of them said anything after.

Mrs. Wincock stood in the doorway as I made the excruciating journey down the pebbled walkway to the Bronco, feeling her pitying eyes like a target on my back. The entire way, I whispered the name of Guidry's fiancée and soon-to-be bride over and over again. *Monica . . . Monica . . . Monica . . . Monica . . .*

By the time I got behind the wheel, I'd said it so many times it didn't seem like an appropriate name for a human being at all—more like a species of lizard, or maybe a topical ointment for ringworm . . . *Ask your doctor about Monica!*

Just as I stabbed my keys into the ignition, Mr. Wincock appeared, his face grim as I rolled down the window. He was still holding the TV remote in one hand, and the laugh lines around his eyes had fallen.

He said, "Miss Dixie, I think you better come see this."

15

As Mr. Wincock led me inside the house, Mrs. Wincock was standing slack-jawed in the middle of the living room, just next to the tarp of harpsichord innards, her arms hanging limply at her sides, her eyes fixed on the TV screen. She turned and said, "Oh, dear."

The reporter had perfectly coiffed brunette hair perched on top of her head like a lacquered helmet. She was gesturing at the scene behind her, which at first looked like nothing more than an empty roadside with a dense woods behind it, but then the camera panned around to reveal a deputy squad car, its lights flashing blue and red.

The reporter stepped into the frame and nodded earnestly. "What we know so far is that a morning jogger was making his way down this peaceful stretch of road when he was nearly run down by a car that came speeding out of this driveway. It took off toward the center of town. We don't know yet what kind of car it was, but as soon as we get more details we'll let you know."

All I could think was how impossibly overinflated the woman's breasts were. They seemed to defy all reason and logic, squeezed as they were into an impossibly tight silvery blouse like two Goodyear blimps floating side by side in front of her body. I wondered that they didn't each have their own LED display panel, with blinking text announcing the end of dignified reporting as we know it. Surely, I thought to myself, this was not what Mr. Wincock wanted me to see.

I said, "What's happening?"

He said, "A jogger found a dead body on a private lane." He turned to me. "They said it's down on the south end of the Key."

I nodded.

"They said it's off Midnight Pass . . . by Turtle Beach."

Just then, the reporter pointed to the driveway beyond the squad car, and I felt the hair on the back of my neck stand up.

Mrs. Wincock said, "Dixie, didn't you say you live down there?"

I'd like to think I said something like, "Okay, thanks for letting me know," or, at the very least, "I need to go now," but I don't remember saying a word. I'd also like to think I turned and walked calmly around Mr. Wincock's harpsichord project and then made my way out the front door with measured aplomb, but I didn't. I stormed right through all the various piles of parts and burst through the front door like a bat out of hell, where I collided into Deputy Marshall so hard it nearly toppled him to the ground.

Blocking my way, he said, "Miss Hemingway, where are you going?"

I said, "I need to get home."

He held his hands out in front of me like he was calming a rabid dog. "Now, hold on. I just received a request to keep you here until we know exactly what's happening."

My eyes must have looked like they were about to pop out of my head, because he immediately took one step back and said, "Okay. Let's don't panic."

I looked down at the ground and thought for a moment. I was beginning to think somebody in the sheriff's office had given Marshall a heads-up about me. I repeated myself, trying to keep my voice as calm as possible, "I need. To get. *Home.*"

That stretch of road behind the reporter on the TV— I had recognized it almost immediately. The sea grape and moss-laden oaks should have been a dead giveaway, but as soon as I saw the rusty old PRIVATE DRIVEWAY sign that sits at the top of our lane, my body had switched into autopilot.

Marshall adjusted his belt. "I think it'll be safer for everyone involved if we wait right here until further notice. Got it?"

I said, "That's a great idea. You do that."

I steered past him and headed for the Bronco, but I

hadn't gotten far when I felt his hand on my left shoulder. I spun around to face him, knocking his arm out of the way.

I said, "Deputy, everyone left on this earth that I care about is in that house. I'm going there now. You can help me, or you can arrest me for speeding when we get there." I hadn't felt this mix of rage and fear in a very long time. Every muscle in my body was as tightly drawn as a cat poised for attack, but when I spoke, my voice was calm and even. *"Got it?"*

I didn't even look back.

I jumped in the Bronco and fired the engine. Pulling out of the driveway, I caught a glimpse of Mr. and Mrs. Wincock in their doorway. Mrs. Wincock had Mrs. Heedles in her arms, and they were all three watching me, motionless and wide-eyed, like they were watching the climactic scene of a horror movie.

I screeched to a stop at the corner of the main road and took a deep breath, telling myself to keep my eyes open and my wits about me. I knew I wouldn't be doing anybody any favors if I crashed and burned trying to get there, and I certainly didn't want to put anybody else in danger, but every cell in my body was telling me to get home as fast as possible, no matter the cost.

Just then, a blur of colored lights streamed by on my left, and the next thing I knew Marshall's squad car was in the middle of the intersection, with cars in both directions rolling to a stop as the wail of his siren broke through the deafening buzz in my head. Marshall leaned out his window and pointed directly at me. Then, as if cracking an imaginary whip, he signaled me to follow, and I stepped on the gas.

With Marshall leading the way, I'm pretty sure we shot through town faster than anyone's ever driven from one end of the island to the other. Less than two minutes later, we'd gone through the traffic light at Stickney Point, where there was a line of cars in front of us about a half mile long, like a stalled parade headed south. There wasn't room enough on the shoulder to pass them, so Marshall veered into the oncoming lane, his lights and sirens shifting into full-out emergency mode. From then on, we had a clear path.

There were no cars coming north.

At some point, my field of vision narrowed to a deep, dark tunnel, as if I was peering through the ragged aperture of a homemade pinhole camera and all I could see were the flashing lights of Marshall's cruiser in front of me. Everything else turned black and fuzzy around the edges. I kept hearing Michael say he was going for a jog, and how Paco had said he'd noticed a rabbit's nest along the driveway and that he had some carrot tops for them. As we got closer, I caught the occasional glimpse of people gathered outside their cars or standing on the sidewalk, craning their necks to see what in the world was happening up ahead.

I saw the news van first, bathed in a sea of emergency lights. There was a cameraman with his back against the hood, his handheld video camera perched on his shoulder, an unlit cigarette dangling from his mouth, and the brunette reporter I'd seen on the Wincocks' television screen was checking her lipstick in the reflection of the van's back window.

As Deputy Marshall rolled up, I pulled in behind him and immediately jumped out, not even bothering to cut the engine. There were two sheriff's cars on either side of our driveway, and a couple of Sarasota police officers holding traffic. I realized Deputy Marshall must have radioed ahead and requested they keep the northbound lane closed until we arrived.

I hadn't gotten ten feet when someone grabbed me from behind. It was Michael, dressed in the same shorts and tank top he was wearing that morning, and the sight of him nearly made me collapse right there in the road. Before I could even get a word out, he stopped me.

"Okay. We're all fine. Ethan and Paco are down at the house talking to the cops right now."

I said, "What happened?"

"I don't know yet. Somebody was jogging by and they almost got run down by a car coming out of our lane. That's when he noticed something about midway down to the house . . . it's a body."

I said, "You saw it?"

"Yeah." He paused, his eyes going glassy. "It's a woman. Blond. Right in the middle of the lane by the magnolia. There's blood."

I felt pressure beginning to build in the space behind my eyes as I struggled for words. "I just . . . I don't believe it. I was at a client's house, and I saw it on the news. I didn't . . . I didn't know who it was. I thought . . ."

The idea that somebody might have been stalking me was hard enough to deal with, but it paled in comparison to the idea that someone might have hurt Michael or Paco or Ethan. Michael grabbed me around the shoulders and hugged me tight.

He said, "Yeah, well if you think that was bad . . . imagine what I thought."

I pulled away. There were tears in his bloodshot eyes. "Oh, Michael . . ."

He hugged me again. "Okay. Alright, we're fine. Let's just not think about it."

"Yeah, yeah. Okay, yeah." I could feel my body reeling as the adrenaline began to catch up with me. "I think I better sit down."

We went over to the side of the road and found a spot in the grass opposite the driveway. They were letting a slow trickle of traffic through now, and I felt like a monkey in a cage as the cars rolled by, the passengers inside gawking at us. The sky overhead was bright blue, with two mountain-size white clouds gliding east to west, as if nothing was happening at all and everything was perfectly fine in the universe. We sat there in silence, watching the various officers milling around, coming and going up the lane from our house.

Finally, after what seemed like an eternity, I turned to Michael and said, "Why is this happening?"

He shook his head and sighed. "I wish I knew."

"I mean, there's no way, right?"

"No way . . . what?"

I waved my hand around. "All this. There's no way it's a coincidence."

His eyes stopped on a spot across the road, and I could tell by his face he'd already been thinking the exact same thing. First, Sara Potts, with my name on her body, and now . . . not three hundred feet from our front door . . .

Michael said, "Okay. Let's not jump to any conclusions until we know exactly what's going on."

I looked up to see a trio of men coming around the curve of our driveway. It was only then that I noticed the shape in the middle of the lane, about a hundred yards down. It was too far to see clearly, but there were two deputies carefully unfolding a blue tarp, which I figured was meant to protect the body until a forensics team arrived to investigate.

I could tell by his profile that one of the men coming toward us was Paco, and despite the fact that Michael had already told me he was fine, I felt a muscle in the middle of my throat let go at the sight of him. As they passed the spot where the body was, he kept his face turned. One of the men stopped, and now it was just Paco coming up the lane, along with another taller, skinnier man. It took me a second to realize who it was: Matthew Carthage, the blond boy-detective I'd met in front of Caroline's house, wearing the same faded jeans and white oxford dress shirt. I looked around for Detective McKenzie's unmarked SUV but couldn't find it.

Paco had a canvas shopping bag from our local health-food store slung over his shoulder. He walked across the road and straight into my arms, hugging me as Michael mutely patted both our backs. I could tell he was struggling to keep it all together, but I tried not to let on. It's important for Michael to feel he has things under control, especially in a situation like this.

Detective Carthage was standing a few feet back, typing something into his cell phone.

I scanned Paco's face. "Who is she?"

He shook his head. "They don't know yet. I didn't recognize her at all. Middle-aged, white, nicely dressed. There's no purse or ID or anything . . ."

"Where's Ethan?"

"Looking for Ella. She's hiding, probably just freaked out by all the activity, or by what happened here. Whatever it was . . ." His voice trailed away as he glanced first at Detective Carthage, then at Michael.

Michael's eyes narrowed. "What?"

Carthage stepped forward and cleared his throat, his neck suddenly breaking out in splotches of scarlet as he leveled me with his pale green eyes.

"There's another note."

16

When I was a kid, my grandfather liked to tell me bedtime stories about the people who lived here before us. My grandmother would lay my pajamas out while I was brushing my teeth—sometimes posing them on the bed, their arms relaxed over the pillow and their legs all akimbo. Once I was tucked in, my grandfather would come upstairs and slide a chair over to the bed. More often than not, Michael would sneak in and lay on the rug to listen, even though he was older and much too sophisticated for such childish things.

Usually the stories began with the brave Miccosukee or the noble Seminole Indians, descendants of the indigenous people that roamed our shores long before anyone knew there would ever be a thing called Florida. He told stories of mighty battles—struggles with neighboring tribes and clashes with Europeans and Spaniards—all mixed in with woolly mammoths and wild brontosauruses grazing in the fields, cavemen throwing giant parties, and Neanderthals dancing around roaring campfires where giant tortoises grilled in their own shells.

For the longest time, I bought those stories hook, line, and sinker. I took it for granted that our European settlers rode through the dunes on the backs of saber-toothed tigers, and I'm ashamed to admit that I was nearly a teenager before I figured out it was all pure fabrication on my grandfather's part.

But it didn't matter. I loved the rich world my grandfather wove for us kids, and even if it wasn't all factually true, he somehow managed to capture the strange, wild essence of Florida's character. Sometimes, he'd skip forward a few thousand years and talk about the eccentric family that owned our little stretch of beach right before we came along. According to my grandfather, they were the distant cousins of Nelson Rockefeller, as well as the illegitimate children of a glamorous and beautiful circus performer known as Minerva, who was rumored to have traveled Europe as the "personal assistant" to John Jacob Astor.

Now, this should all be taken with a grain of salt, because as I understand it, they traveled from country to country in a convoy of hot-air balloons, held aloft with the breath of fire-breathing dragons ... In other words, don't sue me if any of this turns out to be less than accurate. But apparently Minerva and John Jacob Astor had twenty children, all of whom spent their later years living together not far from here in a giant mansion made of imported Italian marble. The eldest, Paolo, was a botanist. His particular field of interest was the

Talauma plumieri, or what you and I know as the magnolia tree.

He planted them all over the island, and, if my grandfather is to be believed, all the existing wild magnolias on the Key are direct descendants of those very trees.

I was thinking about that as Michael and Paco and I followed Detective Carthage down the shelled lane that leads to our house. Before we even got close, I could feel the heady nectar of the magnolia's cupped blossoms on the back of my throat, and for a brief moment, something about the smell of it, the thickness of it, combined with the idea of a dead body nearby, made my head swoon. I put a hand on Michael's shoulder to steady myself. The whole thing didn't feel real . . . more like a bizarre, fever-induced nightmare.

When Detective Carthage had said there was "another note," I'd just stood there, staring at him in silence. All kinds of questions started bouncing around in my head like ping-pong balls in a lottery machine, but I didn't say a word. For one, I wasn't sure I wanted to know the answers, and, two, I could tell by the bewildered expression on Detective Carthage's face that there were still a lot of details he hadn't figured out yet. He was probably waiting for Detective McKenzie to show up before he made any further decisions.

The body had been covered with a blue tarp, the four corners pinned down with metal spikes, and as we walked by I took my cue from Paco and kept my head turned away from the mounded form in the middle. Instead, I focused on the magnolia tree, where Paco had seen the rabbit's nest that morning. There were a few fan-leafed palms jutting out at angles from its base, and nestled among them was a dense collection of dried grasses and twigs with a dark hollow near the center. I wondered why a mother rabbit would choose to raise her babies so close to the edge of the driveway.

After we were well past the body, I realized I'd been holding my breath and gulped for air. Detective Carthage's shoulders were slumped forward, like he was trying to compensate for his tall, lanky frame, and with every step his blond bangs swept across his forehead like windshield wipers. It was only then that I noticed he was mumbling to himself—or at least that's what I thought— but then I realized he was actually talking to Michael, who was walking next to him on the other side.

I moved in closer to listen.

Michael said, "But . . . are you sure?"

Carthage said, "Not a hundred percent, no. Obviously, we'll have a better idea when we see what's written on that note, if anything, but I don't want to touch it until the body's been examined."

I noticed the bright blue fingertips of a rubber glove peaking out of his back pocket, so I wasn't totally sure I believed he hadn't already looked at the note, but I decided to play along for now. I was about to ask if he knew when Detective McKenzie would be here, especially since I was beginning to worry about all the pets I still had to take care of, but Carthage interrupted. "So how long do you think you and Paco were gone?"

Michael thought for a second. "Not even an hour. Probably no more than half an hour, actually."

Detective Carthage nodded. "So you went for a walk down the beach, and you left together?"

"Yes."

"And which direction did you go?"

"South, down to the end of Turtle Beach. There were some kids flying a kite, so we went down and watched them for a little while, and then we headed back. That's when the cops showed up."

"A little while?"

"Maybe half an hour or so."

"And before you left, you didn't hear a car coming up the driveway or anything like that?"

Michael shook his head. "No, definitely not."

"And was there anyone else on the beach?"

"Nobody. Just us and those kids."

Suddenly, I stopped dead in my tracks. "Wait a minute! Where's Gigi?"

Paco stepped over and slid the canvas shopping bag off his shoulder. "I figured you'd think of that eventually."

He opened it up to reveal Gigi huddled inside, his little head and ears poking out of a tumble of underwear and mismatched socks from my top dresser drawer.

Paco shrugged meekly, "We knew you'd freak out if we left him in the house alone. I grabbed whatever was nearby."

I almost burst out laughing, but instead a sob come rushing up my throat. I took a deep breath and reached in to give Gigi a reassuring rub between the ears, but he tensed at my touch and burrowed further into his little bed of underwear. I took the bag from Paco and lifted it gently over my shoulder.

I said, "I know, buddy. I'll be glad when this is over too."

Detective Carthage continued. "The main thing now is to figure out who this woman is so we can at least tell her family and see if they know anything. I'm hoping they might be able to explain the connection to the other body."

I stopped again. "What other body?"

"Sara Potts? Remember her?"

"Sorry. I thought you meant another body *here*."

Carthage shook his head almost imperceptibly, like he'd already considered that possibility. He said, "We ran the plates. Now we're just waiting to see if they can identify a cell phone number."

I could feel pressure building behind my eyes, and a throbbing pain was slowly creeping its way across my shoulders as all the muscles in my neck started to tighten.

Michael said, "Dixie, what's wrong?"

I said, "Can somebody please explain to me what the hell is going on? What cell phone? And what do you mean you ran the plates? What plates?"

Paco said, "When we got back from our walk, there was a car parked in your spot in the carport. We looked everywhere, but we couldn't find anybody, and that's when the deputies showed up and said a jogger had reported a woman in the driveway."

Carthage said, "The plates are registered to a rental company here at the airport. They gave us the name of the people that rented the car and their phone number too, except it's a landline. They didn't leave a cell phone number. That means unless they check their home messages, we won't be able to reach anybody . . . at least until they figure out somebody's missing."

I said, "What about the note . . . where is it?"

"It's pinned to her blouse."

I could feel myself starting to get a little light-headed again. I mumbled, "It's pinned to her blouse . . ."

Carthage said, "Yes, ma'am."

"Let me guess . . . with a hat pin."

He nodded slowly. "Yeah. With a black pearl at the tip."

I paused for a moment, suddenly filled with an overwhelming desire to turn around and walk right back up to the main road and drive away. First of all, there were pets all over the Key depending on me to take care of them, but also, I didn't want to know what that note said. It couldn't have been anything good.

I tried to keep my cool. "So, when does Detective McKenzie get here?"

Carthage said, "She doesn't."

"Huh?"

Michael glanced at Paco as Carthage turned and headed for the house. "She's out of town for a couple days. New Orleans, I think."

Michael and Paco both followed him, their eyes on the ground and not saying a word. Detective Carthage kept on talking, but his words floated over my head without registering, as if my brain had taken in all the information it could handle for one day and had hung up an OUT TO LUNCH sign. I caught a few words here and there, like "old friend" and "wedding," but that was about it.

As we turned the corner of the lane and our house came into view, I saw Ethan standing at the bottom of the steps to my apartment. He had Ella Fitzgerald cradled in his arms, and now I really did feel like I would burst into tears . . . until I saw the car parked in the carport behind him. It was a giant SUV, and even at this distance, I recognized it right away.

Just then, one of the deputies trotted up to Detective Carthage. He said, "Sir, we found this."

He was holding out a small plastic bag. Inside was a cigarette, the tip of which was smudged with pink.

Detective Carthage said, "Okay, hold on to that. We'll see if it matches the lipstick on the body. Where'd you find it?"

He started to answer but I interrupted him. I'd seen the woman throw it in the driveway myself.

I said, "Reed."

Detective Carthage turned to me. "What?"

"Reed. That's the name on the rental car, isn't it?"

His brow furrowed. "How do you know that?"

I could feel a dark, sinking feeling settling into my body as an image flashed in my mind: Edith Reed, rising out of her car the morning she and her husband had wandered around our property. I could still see the gleam of the tennis bracelet on her wrist, with its matching diamond pendants dangling from her ears.

I said, "Because they were here. Two days ago."

"Who was here?"

"Garth and Edith Reed." I tipped my chin at the green SUV parked in my spot. "That's their car."

Michael's jaw dropped open, and for a split second I wondered what my grandfather would make of the story that was currently unfolding on the very spot where he and my grandmother had built their lives . . . and whether or not he'd buy it.

I reached into my back pocket and pulled out the little piece of yellow paper I'd found wedged under my car seat.

"And here's their cell phone number."

17

It was her.

Mrs. Reed.

Detective Carthage wanted me to confirm beyond a shadow of a doubt that she was the same woman I'd seen the other morning, and I knew it would have been ludicrous to refuse. The woman's face had lost the smoothness I remembered when I'd spied her from my hiding place in the hammock. Now, it had loosened and sagged, the skin of her left cheek almost melting into the crushed shell of the driveway, her silvery blond hair flattened on one side. I nodded quietly, and then Detective Carthage pulled the tarp back over her face.

I didn't want to be there when her husband arrived, but, still, it was hard to drive away. Except for Ella, I was the only female left on the scene. Silly, I know. Such a small thing. I hadn't known Mrs. Reed. I couldn't have saved her.

Still, it felt like a betrayal, to leave with all those strangers stepping around her body. Less than three hours earlier, she'd been touring the Key without a care in the world, scoping out potential sites for her future home, and now she was on her side, under a blue plastic tarp littered with fallen magnolia petals, while a crowd of technicians, deputies, photographers, and investigators milled about, talking quietly and making notes. Sipping at their coffees. But mostly, and I'm ashamed to admit it, I didn't want to see the look on her husband's face when he saw her—*really* saw her—for the last time.

I know what that's like, and it's no fun.

In exchange for letting me get back to work, Detective Carthage had asked that I meet him later, which I readily agreed to at the time, but I was already trying to come up with ways to get out of it. I didn't much feel like talking to anybody, at least not any humans.

Luckily, I had a stable of cats waiting to help distract me . . .

Betty and Grace Piker are two retired sisters who've come to a mutual agreement. If one of them finds a cat that needs a home and wants to adopt it, the other is to do everything in her power to prevent it, including physical force if necessary. Fortunately, at least for homeless cats everywhere, the Piker sisters' resolve is as weak as their hearts are large. They have ten cats, all rescues, and they'd recently added yet another feline to the family: an elderly calico named Lucy.

As soon as I opened the door, I heard a furry-footed stampede coming up the hallway from the kitchen, and then I spent a good ten minutes rolling around on the floor greeting everybody. Then they all scampered after me into the kitchen, where I slid my backpack off my shoulder and zipped it open a little further. Gigi was inside, half-asleep in his makeshift bed of socks and underwear.

"You okay in there?"

He wriggled his nose, which I took to mean yes, and then I propped the bag up on one of the bar chairs, looping the shoulder straps over the chair to secure it. The cats' food supplies were lined up on the counter next to the refrigerator, which was covered with family photos—class pictures and wedding shots—along with roughly a thousand refrigerator magnets. One read, MAKE YOUR-SELF AT HOME: CLEAN MY KITCHEN. Another displayed a cheerful woman in a red bandanna, holding a slice of chocolate pie to her lips. The caption read, STRESSED IS DESSERTS SPELLED BACKWARDS.

I thought about sitting down right there on the floor and wasting an hour or two reading them all, but I knew those cats wouldn't be too happy with me if I did that, plus I still had lots of other pets to tend to. I prepared ten individual bowls of kibble with a little bit of warm water, then I distributed them all around the kitchen so everybody had enough room to eat in private. Then I did a thorough run-through of the house and found Lucy in one of the bedrooms, sunning herself on a windowsill.

When I came in, she rose up on all fours, pressing the tips of her toes down and arching her back, purring like a tiny storm generator as I ran my fingers from the scruff of her neck to the tip of her tail, leaving little furrows in her plush, silky fur. I bent down and pressed my forehead into hers.

She said, "*Thrrrrp* . . . ?"

I said, "Yes, ma'am."

I'd brought her bowl with me, specially prepared with her prescription senior kibble, plus a little canned wet food on top to make it extra tempting. As I put it down on the carpet, she hopped off the sill and took a few dainty bites. I sat down on the edge of the bed and sighed. I knew I needed to give the Wincocks a call. I realized I'd left them so abruptly, and I was pretty sure those reporters had probably broadcast video of Michael and me sitting on the side of the road outside the crime scene.

Mrs. Wincock answered on the first ring.

"Dixie, are you okay?"

"I'm totally fine. I just wanted to apologize for running out of there so fast. That private lane where they found the body . . ."

She said, "I know, we saw everything on the news. Do you know who she was?"

"A tourist, visiting the island looking for a place to buy. But I just called to let you know I'll be at your house tomorrow to take care of Mrs. Heedles just like we planned."

I heard a sigh of relief. "Oh, that's good to hear. I knew you'd call if there was a problem. We leave for New Orleans bright and early in the morning."

I said, "Okay, well, have a good time at the . . ."

I stopped myself from saying the word *wedding* and opted for "trip" instead.

She hesitated. "Dixie . . . if you need to talk, you know you can call me anytime."

I wasn't sure what she meant by that, so I just said, "Okay, sounds good!" and hung up the phone.

By then, Lucy had scarfed up all her food and was sitting next to me on the bed, gazing into my eyes and kneading my thigh with her paws. I usually don't have to worry about spending a ton of time with the Piker cats, mainly because there are so many of them they do a perfectly fine job of keeping each other entertained, but Lucy seemed to be taking a little longer getting used to her new family.

I cupped her chin in the palm of my hand and said, "Let's go take a look at the pond."

She padded after me into the kitchen, where I shook my head thinking about Mrs. Wincock's offer. What did she mean, *if I needed to talk*? Talk about what? Guidry? Did she think I cared? That I gave a rat's ass about that stupid wedding? That I'd want her to report what Guidry's tuxedo looked like, or the flower arrangements, or how many people were there, or what the cake looked like, or whether Monochrome had chosen to wear a white gown?

No, thank you.

I shook my head again as I washed all the kitty bowls and put the supplies away. I shook my head some more as I led everybody out to the backyard, and then I shook my head at least two or three more times while I gave Lucy a good grooming. We sat in the grass next to the pond. I ran the brush through her coat, removing enough fur to stuff a small pillow, and we watched the goldfish patrol the water's edge in languid circles while the other cats hunted around the fenced perimeter for crickets and butterflies.

When we were done, Lucy headed back to her spot on the windowsill in the bedroom. I told her I'd stop by again later, giving her a kiss on the nose as a little thank-you for cheering me up a bit. I left everybody else napping in a furry pile on the couch in the living room.

After that, I found myself driving aimlessly down Ocean Boulevard with one hand on the wheel and the other tucked inside my backpack on the passenger seat, absentmindedly massaging the scruff of Gigi's neck. I realized I had absolutely no idea where I was headed.

I pulled over to the side of the road and sighed as Deputy Marshall pulled in behind me. If ever there was a possibility that my twenty-four-hour escort might have been relieved of his duties, I knew it had been completely eliminated the moment that poor woman's body had been discovered in my driveway. Detective Carthage had been adamant—I wasn't to be left alone for one second.

Marshall got out of his car and trotted up to my window. "You okay?"

I waved him away. "Yeah, I'm fine. I just needed to make a phone call."

He took a couple of steps back. "Okay, sorry. Just checking."

I pulled my phone out of the cup holder in the center console and flipped it open as he made his way back, but I didn't need to make a phone call. I needed to get focused before I went on with my day.

I paged through the contacts on my phone, absentmindedly looking for something, anything, that might take my mind off things. Caroline's name appeared. They still hadn't gotten ahold of her, but Detective Carthage had insisted I not call her again until they had a chance to talk to her first. I was worried sick about her, but I tried not to think about it. I told myself she was fine and kept scrolling.

The name of my favorite haunt rolled by—the Village Diner, which for all intents and purposes is my home away from home—but the thought of stopping by for a cup of coffee made my heart sink. Judy, the diner's only full-time waitress, is probably my closest friend, and Tanisha, the cook there, is like a sister. I knew I couldn't face them without blabbing out everything that had happened . . . and I wasn't sure I felt like reliving it just yet.

Then, Guidry's name rolled by, summoning more questions about the wedding, which I was beginning to think everybody in this damn town was attending except me.

I looked at myself in the rearview mirror and muttered, "What in the world is wrong with you?"

Two women had lost their lives, and here I was fretting about an old flame getting married. What was it? *Jealousy?* First of all, what a dirty, low-down thing to do to Ethan, the man who loved me now, who accepted me for who I was, who didn't go away. And second, it wasn't like Guidry had run off with another woman. Our undoing had been just as much my decision as his.

Enough, I told myself. There were a lot more important things to worry about. At that, the image of poor Mrs. Reed's face appeared, and then slowly fading into view was Sara Potts. I realized with a jolt that I had no idea if Sara's family had been contacted yet. Would they want to meet me? Would they want to know the details of what I had witnessed? And would Mr. Reed want to talk to me too? I was, after all, the last person on earth to have seen both their loved ones alive.

And then I looked at myself in the rearview mirror and took a deep breath.

No.

I wasn't the last person to see them *alive* . . .

That was someone else.

18

Detective Carthage had asked me to meet him at the Siesta Pavilion, a little covered courtyard at the edge of the beach where there's a collection of long picnic tables, a tiny gift shop that sells beach toys and cheap souvenirs, and a snack bar. I knew it was no coincidence—it was the very same snack bar where Sara Potts had worked until two days ago.

The place was filled to the brim with kids in board shorts and bikinis, all running around in the sun, wet, barefoot, and chattering like wild monkeys. If it hadn't been that Carthage was dressed in his regulation faded jeans and white oxford button-down, I might not have been able to tell him apart from all the other fresh-faced teenagers.

I spotted him on the far side closest to the beach. As I wound my way through the tables with the smell of fast food wafting up around me, I realized with a groan I'd barely eaten a thing all day long. I wondered what Detective Carthage would think if I grabbed a hot dog and a couple baskets of curly fries to wolf down during our meeting, but I managed to control myself.

As I slid into the bench opposite him, he pulled out two file folders from his briefcase and laid them on the table in front of me.

He said, "Hi, Mrs. Hemingway."

"You can call me Dixie."

There was an awkward pause, and for some stupid reason I felt compelled to keep on talking. "Being called *Mrs. Hemingway* just makes me feel like an old lady . . ."

I added a lighthearted laugh, but the noise that came out of me sounded more like the bleat of a guinea pig (or an old lady). I cleared my throat and told myself to shut the hell up. Why in the world I was so nervous in the presence of a kid almost young enough to be my own son was beyond me.

Just then, two teenage girls, one blond and one brunette, walked by in bikini bottoms and matching tie-dyed T-shirts. One was carrying a plastic tray from the snack bar, piled high with fries and onion rings, and the other had a giant candy-striped beach umbrella balanced on one shoulder.

"Matt?"

Both girls stopped in their tracks.

Detective Carthage looked up and immediately blushed. "Oh, hey."

The blond said, "OMG Matthew Carthage? What are you doing here? Didn't you move to Harvard or something?"

He nodded. "Princeton, yeah, but I'm back now."

She glanced briefly at me and then frowned. "You dropped out?"

"Uh. No, I graduated already."

She flashed him a goofy grin and rolled her eyes. "Yeah, right. Wanna come hang out with us?"

Carthage turned to me and said, "Well, we're kind of in the middle of something here . . ."

The brunette, the one with the umbrella, held up one hand and waved it at me, kind of like a beauty pageant princess on a parade float. "Hi. Sorry to interrupt. I'm Alison and this is Kerry. We went to high school with Matt, but for some reason they wouldn't let us go to Harvard."

The blond girl giggled. "Yeah, I can't imagine why, but I guess we can't all be geniuses. We're juniors at Florida State."

I said, "Oh, cool. Nice to meet you both."

She said, "Yeah, must be nice to have Matt home for the summer, huh?"

I gulped. "Yeah, it sure is . . ."

She gave me a polite, pitying smile that teenagers reserve for their elders and then turned her attention back to Matthew.

"Well, we'll be down by the volleyball courts if you change your mind and wanna come hang out with the dumb kids for a change."

She wrinkled her nose and gave him a wink.

He stammered, "Okay, yeah, sure."

As they made their way, the brunette twirled her umbrella at me. "Nice to meet you, Mrs. Carthage!"

I gave her a thumbs-up and said, "You bet!"

Inside my head, I'm not much older than seventeen, so it's always a bit of a shock to the system whenever I'm reminded of the ugly truth. In fact, it was all I could do to keep from leaping off my seat and attacking the child with her own umbrella, but given the fact that a homicide detective was sitting right across the table from me, I figured I'd better keep my mouth shut and my butt in the seat.

Detective Carthage's face had turned bright pink. "Sorry about that."

I said, "OMG it's totally fine."

He blushed. "Maybe we better move somewhere more private . . ."

"Good idea," I said. "You gather up your files and I'll get my walker."

We moved over to a bench just a little ways up the beach but more deserted, and as soon as we sat down, Carthage said, "Before I forget, we found Caroline Greaver."

I gasped. "You did?"

"This morning. She's in Key West. She's apparently having a wonderful vacation. And you were right about her phone, it died and she didn't have a charger with her."

I must have looked like I'd just been hit over the head with a sledgehammer. "So . . . she's okay?"

He nodded. "I explained everything that's happened, so she was a little shocked, of course. She asked me to thank you for taking care of her pets, and that she'll call as soon as she can get her phone charged up."

A feeling of relief washed over my body. I realized

this entire time I'd feared the worst . . . that somehow Caroline had gotten mixed up in all of this . . . that she'd found herself in the path of the killer.

I said, "Wait . . . if her phone is still dead, how in the world did you find her?"

"I'm a detective. That's what I do."

A small smile appeared on his lips as he laid a file on the bench between us. Clipped to the top was a photocopy of a driver's license. I recognized the woman in the photo right away. It was Edith Reed.

Carthage said, "This is the woman who visited your house that morning with her husband, right?"

I sighed. "Yeah. That's her."

"We found her license in the bushes about twenty feet from the car. Her purse was nearby. Apparently, she decided to stop by your house again, alone, to see if anybody was home. She took a walk down your driveway, and that's when someone stabbed her." He glanced at me. "The same as Sara Potts."

I closed my eyes. "Until now, I had no idea how Sara Potts had died."

"If it's any consolation. Neither of them would have seen it coming. They probably both died quickly."

"And what about the man across the street?"

He frowned. "What man?"

"Rupert Wolff. The man I saw on Caroline's front porch."

He shook his head dismissively. "No. We looked into that. He's just visiting, but there's something else I need to tell you. It's about Edith Reed."

Almost immediately I pictured her, lying in my

driveway surrounded with magnolia petals. I felt my jaw tighten. "It's about the other note, isn't it?"

"Yeah . . ."

"Did it have my name on it too?"

"No."

His gaze was fixed on the group of teenagers playing volleyball down by the water's edge. I couldn't tell from this far away, but I figured his two high school friends were probably among them. Just before Carthage answered, I heard one of the kids call out, "Nice shot!"

Detective Carthage looked down at his hands.

"It said, *Third time's a charm.*'"

19

Here's how they make a spicy grapefruit margarita at Colonel Teddy's Tiki Bar on Siesta Key:

Take a fresh habañero pepper, cut it in half, and then steep it in three ounces of Pueblo Viejo tequila. Next, add an ounce of freshly squeezed lime juice, an ounce of freshly squeezed grapefruit juice, and then one ounce of simple syrup plus a couple handfuls of crushed ice. Cover and shake it for no less than thirty seconds and then immediately pour it, ice and all, into a mason jar with a salted rim, garnished with a wedge of key lime or meyer lemon or both.

You can specify how hot you like it.

For example, if you ask for "pleasantly spicy," they'll drop the pepper in a cocktail shaker, pour in the tequila, and then remove the pepper immediately. If you ask for "taste-bud abusive," they'll let the pepper sit with the tequila for a couple of minutes. Ask for "medical supervision advised," and they'll use a safely guarded reserve that's been steeping for who knows how long.

And here's how you drink a spicy grapefruit margarita at Colonel Teddy's Tiki Bar on Siesta Key: as slowly as possible.

It's preferable to kick your sandals off and dig your toes in the sand, and if you really want to do it right, you swivel around in your stool and turn your face to the sun to watch the waves roll in. Traditionally, you wait until at least 5:00 P.M., but here in Siesta Key, things are a bit more laid back, so it wouldn't be considered a crime at four. If you happen to have a serial killer on your tail, 3:45 is perfectly acceptable.

After I left my meeting with Detective Carthage, the rest of the day felt like a blur. I'd seen to all my pets—that much I remember. And I remember when I got home our driveway was still cordoned off with police tape, so I had to leave my car on the side of the road. Mrs. Reed's body had already been removed and taken to the county coroner's office by then, but I couldn't bring myself to walk down the lane. Instead, I thrashed my way through the woods with Deputy Marshall following about ten yards behind me, and then I walked along the beach to the house. Marshall sat on the porch all night long, despite Ethan's protests, but to be honest I think he was secretly as happy as I was to have an armed deputy guarding us overnight.

I stirred my finger around in my margarita.

So, someone is trying to kill you.

I nodded, as if I'd come up with something completely brilliant.

Well, isn't that just wonderful?

I nodded again. It seemed almost too outrageous, too

surreal, to be true. And why? Was there something I was missing? Some detail that would explain it all? I knew if I could only connect the two murders I'd have an answer. The problem, of course, was that the only discernible connection between Sara Potts and Edith Reed . . . was me.

The messages on those two notes were playing in my head like a broken record: *See you in hell, Dixie . . . Third time's a charm . . . See you in hell, Dixie . . . Third time's a charm . . .* I opened my eyes and realized I was talking out loud. At a nearby table was a young couple sharing a basket of crispy fried shrimp and a large Coke, but they didn't seem to notice, or if they did they were too polite to stare at the crazy lady at the bar, drinking alone in the middle of the day and mumbling to herself. A few tables away were two salty sea-captain types glaring at each other over a row of empty Budweiser bottles.

I took another sip of my margarita.

It burned my lips, but I didn't care. At this point, anything that distracted me from the reality of the situation was more than welcome. Detective Carthage had contacted Sara Potts's family—they were on their way to town now with the horrible task of identifying her body—and he'd spoken with the staff at the snack bar. The manager there had told him he'd gotten worried when Sara hadn't shown up for work, which was unlike her. She'd always been an excellent employee, dependable and friendly, and he didn't know anybody who might have wanted to hurt her. Still, no one could explain what she was doing in Caroline's house. As far as anyone knew, they hadn't been friends.

I closed my eyes again and tried not to think about it, focusing on the stinging tequila in my throat and the gentle breeze in the air. In a little while, I heard what at first sounded like a flock of chickens in the distance but turned out to be a group of about six elderly ladies in brightly colored print blouses and open-toed sandals making their way toward the bar, all talking and laughing over one another. They wore matching baseball caps embroidered with coral-pink sequins, and I figured they were probably a local gardening club or a reading group out for a field trip. They plopped their purses down in the sand at the opposite end of the bar, and one of them announced, "Now, I'm warning you, ladies. Once I sit down, I may never leave this bar again!"

I had to admit, that sounded like an excellent idea. In fact, I was thinking I might go over and join them for the rest of my life, but then the bartender tapped me on the shoulder.

"What do you say?"

He was suntanned, with a nice smile and tousled blond hair that fell to his shoulders. His tortoiseshell glasses made him look a little older, but I could tell he wasn't much more than twenty-five or so. He wore board shorts with a faded dive-shop T-shirt and a forest-green baseball cap with a yellow bill, tipped jauntily to one side.

I said, "Huh? Sorry, I wasn't listening . . ."

He grinned. "I could tell. You seem pretty lost in thought. Wanna take another stab at it?"

"Another stab at what?"

He waved my empty margarita jar in the air. "At whatever it is you're trying to forget."

"Ha. I'd better not. That's a good line though."

He grinned. "Thanks. I speak fluent bartender."

"Oh, did you study that in college?"

He shook his head. "Actually, no. I'm studying poetry."

"You're a poet?"

He winked. "No. I'm a bartender. Just the check then?"

I nodded as he dropped my glass down into a sink of soapy water and headed over to the women with a handful of menus. A little louder than necessary, he said, "Alright girls, I'm gonna need to see some IDs," and they all giggled appreciatively.

There was a pink plastic caddy on the bar in front of me with various drink garnishes. I looked for something to give Gigi, who was sitting in a red plastic tortilla chip basket perched on the stool next to me, but celery sticks can be deadly for rabbits, and I didn't think he'd care much for a marinated cherry. He was still munching halfheartedly on the carrot stick I'd given him earlier, but I could tell he was ready for something new. Just the sight of his little floppy ears and fuzzy button nose made my spirits lift a little.

I whispered, "Gigi, I continue to be impressed with how laid back you are, considering the circumstances. I'm not sure I'd be so happy riding around all day in somebody's backpack."

He took a bite and munched thoughtfully, holding his

carrot stick like a cigar. I could tell he was probably wondering how much longer before he could go back home.

I said, "Soon . . . hopefully."

A few minutes later the bartender handed me a slip of paper, and I caught a glimpse of dark red splotches on his fingernails. He withdrew his hand and blushed.

He said, "Nice, huh? Nail polish. I promise it's not what you think. Like, I'm not a cross-dresser or anything."

I held my hands up. "No judgments here."

"It's from a party the other night. My girlfriend thought it would be hilarious if I painted my nails too." He scratched on his thumb nail with his right index finger. "It seemed like an awesome idea at the time, but I had no idea how hard it is to get this damn stuff off."

I laughed. "Have you ever heard of a thing called nail-polish remover?"

He shrugged. "Yeah, but my bar knife works just as good. I chip a little more off whenever I get a break."

I winced as I handed him a twenty-dollar bill. "Well, you better be careful. You could hurt yourself."

He handed my twenty back. "We're all good."

"Huh?"

"Already paid for. That's the receipt."

I shook my head. "No. I can't let you do that."

"I didn't."

He pointed over my shoulder at the group of ladies. They were making their way down to the edge of the water with their margaritas. The wind had picked up a bit, and they were all using their free hands to hold down their sequined caps.

The bartender grinned. "They said you looked like you could use some cheering up."

I smiled to myself all the way across the parking lot. Sometimes, it's the little things that make the world feel right again—at least momentarily. As I came around the front bumper of the Bronco, I averted my eyes from the sheriff's cruiser parked next to me. I knew seeing Deputy Marshall's blank face behind his mirrored sunglasses would bum me out again, so instead I kicked off my left sneaker and shook the sand out of it, balancing on one leg to keep my sock off the ground. Then I repeated the whole process on the other shoe.

Just as I was tightening my laces, I felt a presence behind me and then a shadow fell across the pavement. Before my brain could even register what was happening, I thought of Gigi in my backpack and wondered if I could safely set him down before . . .

Without another thought, I reared back and spun around, clenching my car keys between my knuckles like a hawk's talons. Deputy Morgan was standing right behind me, frowning down at a spot on the hood of his cruiser.

"Damn tree sap."

He looked up at me. My eyes were glaring and my right arm was poised over my head like a snake about to strike.

He said, "What the heck are you doing?"

As nonchalantly as possible, I scratched the top of my head with my car keys. "Nothing. What happened to Deputy Marshall?"

He eyed me warily as he opened the car door. "We

had a shift change while you were over there gettin' drunk. Where to now, boss? You done for the day?"

I noticed grains of sand clinging to the edges of his boots as he sat down in the driver's seat, which meant he probably hadn't been waiting in his car. He'd been lurking around the bar, watching me the entire time.

I said, "First of all, I was not getting drunk. I had one tiny margarita. And second of all, no, I'm not done for the day. In fact, I have a meeting with a new client."

"You sure you're okay to drive?"

I put my hands on my hips. "What do I look like? A lightweight?"

He shrugged, the corners of his mouth rising. "I don't wanna pop your balloon, but yeah, a little bit."

I was about to run through the battery of sobriety tests I'd conducted when I was a deputy myself—reciting the alphabet backward, standing on one foot and touching my nose—when a little lightbulb went off in my head.

My eyes widened. *"Balloon!"*

He frowned. "Huh?"

I held up one finger and said, "Hold that thought," and then sprinted across the parking lot as fast as possible. By the time I reached the bar, Morgan had caught up with me.

Wheezing, he bent over and put his hands on his hips. "Dixie, you gotta work with me here! You can't just go runnin' off without warning me first."

I said, "Sorry, I think I just thought of something."

The bartender was straightening up the bar where the group of ladies had been. They were all still down at the water's edge, kicking at the foamy waves and sipping their drinks. When he saw me approaching, he said, "Back for more?"

I shook my head. "I just wanted to ask you something. About that party you mentioned—what did you mean when you said your girlfriend convinced you to paint your fingernails . . . *too*?"

He grinned. "Oh, it was a costume party. They do it every year."

"They?"

"USF. University of Southern Florida. I'm in the English department. It's kind of a tradition. Most people dress up in drag. You know, guys wear dresses and girls wear suits. They've been doing it so long nobody even remembers why, but it's a total blast. You get to meet all the new students."

I turned to Deputy Morgan as his eyes narrowed.

He said, "And when was this party?"

"Like, five nights ago, at a professor's house. He lives right here on the Key."

I could feel the hair slowly rising on the back of my neck. I said, "I'm sorry. I didn't get your name . . . ?"

"Jason."

I took a deep breath. "Jason, was the party on Old Vineyard Lane?"

"Yeah. How'd you know that?"

"And what are your school colors?"

He pointed at his baseball cap. "Green and yellow. Why?"

I nearly stumbled over myself as I backed away, muttering my thanks as I pulled my cell phone out and started dialing. Detective Carthage answered on the first ring.

I said, "Matthew, I mean Detective, I was just talking to the bartender at Colonel Teddy's. He's a student at USF, in the English department, and he told me one of his professors has a party every year. It was five nights ago, and guess where it was? *Old Vineyard Lane.*"

I paused, waiting to see if he might make the connection, but he didn't respond. I said, "Old Vineyard Lane is Caroline's street! And I think that party was just a couple doors down, because I saw a woman taking some balloons down the night before I discovered Sara's body. And the thing is, it was a costume party. A *drag* party. And guess what their school colors are?"

"Green and yellow."

I nodded. "And remember that striped tie Sara Potts was wearing?"

He said, "Green and yellow."

"Right. And Sara told my brother she'd just started graduate school. I think you'd better go talk to that professor right away."

He said, "Good idea. I'm with him now."

Before my brain could catch up, I said, "I think it's possible they weren't after Sara Potts at all. She just happened to be in the wrong place at the wrong . . . wait, did you say you're with him now?"

There was a short pause. "Yes. And you're exactly right. He lives on Old Vineyard Lane, two doors down from Caroline Greaver. Sara Potts was invited to the party, but she never showed up."

"And . . . ?"

There was a short pause. "Is that all?"

I blanched. "Oh. Sorry. I don't mean to tell you how to do your job."

"Not a problem. But one thing: until we find the person responsible for these murders, I think it's probably a good idea that you talk to as few strangers as possible."

I felt a lump form in the base of my throat. "Yeah, of course."

"But feel free to give me a call if you think of anything else."

I said, "Okay . . . uh, keep up the good work."

He said, "Thanks."

And the line went dead.

After our meeting at the Pavilion, Detective Carthage had done his best to convince me not to work for the next few days. To stay home. To sit in my apartment, staring at the TV or the blank wall like a vegetable, waiting for everybody else to figure out what was going on and who was after me.

I wouldn't even consider it. After Todd and Christy died, I'd spent what felt like an entire lifetime holed up in that apartment . . . endless hours hiding from the world, pretending it didn't exist, waiting for it to all end . . . but I'd changed since then. Plus, it was beginning to look like two innocent women had lost their lives because of me, and I knew I'd never be able to live with myself if I just sat by and did nothing. Now was *not* the time to be afraid.

"No," I whispered out loud. "No more."

20

I pulled into the parking lot of the Kitty Haven and waited for Deputy Morgan to roll in next to me, and as soon as he was situated with his coffee thermos and his newspaper, I gave him a nod and grabbed my backpack. As I walked across the parking lot, I could feel the heat rising off the pavement, and I tried to imagine it burning up all my worries and fears like early morning mist. I didn't want to bring all that negative energy inside . . . they don't call it the Kitty *Haven* for nothing.

The decor can only be described as early American brothel. Inside, the walls are paneled in dark walnut, lined with a ragtag collection of sofas and overstuffed armchairs. There's a big picture window in the front facing the street, with brocaded curtains hanging on either side, looped open with thick braided cords and fringed tassels. There are always a few cats stretched out on the windowsill, watching with sleepy eyes as the cars go by, or absentmindedly grooming their paws, waiting for the next treat.

A little bell over the door announced my arrival as a couple of tabbies lolling on one of the sofas looked up and squinted seductively. Marge Preston came bustling in from the back with a trail of at least a dozen cats scampering behind her. She's plump and white-haired with rosy cheeks and dimples, and her pockets are always fully stocked with goodies to keep her charges happy. If I were a cat, I'd follow Marge around too.

She said, "Dixie, you're just in time. I'm a little worried about Franklin." As she spoke, her voice a pleasant soprano, she tossed treats here and there while the cats scattered about like children at a piñata party. "I can't tell if he's lonely or nervous, but he doesn't seem interested in me at all."

I said, "Oh, that's just Franklin. Don't take it personally."

"Well, either way, I think he'll be glad to see you."

Marge never planned on running a cat kennel in her retirement. She took in a few strays after retiring here, and then neighbors started turning up with wild cats they'd found. Before long she was officially the neighborhood "cat lady," eventually building an addition to the back of her house solely for the purpose of taking in more rescues. There are at least a dozen individual rooms, each about three by six feet, lovingly outfitted with used furniture—all donations from customers or garage sale finds. She led me down the hall to the back, talking all the way.

"Wait 'til you see the improvements!"

I said, "Improvements?"

"Yes, ma'am. I tell you, there's an angel out there

somewhere. I don't know who it is, but a couple of months ago we got an envelope in the mailbox, no return address, and no stamp either. Inside was a cashier's check made out to the Kitty Haven!"

My mouth dropped open. "No way."

"Dixie, as the kids say these days, *way!*"

"For how much?"

Her eyes widened. "Ten thousand."

"Ten thousand . . ."

"*Dollars!* Yes, ma'am. I was just as surprised as you are."

"And you have no idea who it's from?"

She shrugged. "Nope. I thought it was some kind of scam or something, but the bank confirmed it was real. They said I could either cash it or wad it up and use it as the most expensive cat toy in history. Well, I'm no dummy. If some rich kook wants to throw his money at my kitties, who am I to judge?"

She stopped at one of the doors that line the back hallway. "Now I can finally get this old rattletrap fixed up proper. And here's the first thing . . ."

She opened the door and pointed inside. All the rooms are furnished exactly the same—a comfy cat bed, a scratching post or two, and a basket of cat toys—but there was something new. Hanging on the wall under the window, at perfect cat's-eye level, was a flat-screen television. It was playing a video of birds flitting around in the branches of a pine tree. Franklin was perched on a little footstool in front of it, completely transfixed.

Marge said, "I know I shouldn't encourage it, but cats are hunters after all. It's in their nature. And I never let them watch the ones with bird feeders—only the birds they could never reach on their own. I'm going out of town for a couple of days, so this'll help keep 'em company."

Marge's assistant, a pretty young girl named Jaz, poked her head in. "She bought one for every room. Apparently, she doesn't think I'm entertaining enough on my own."

Marge clucked at her. "Oh, now hush. You know that's not true. And anyway, wait 'til I'm gone and you'll find out—it's no picnic keeping a small army of cats occupied all by yourself. If it was, I wouldn't need *you*."

Jaz winked, her smile flashing white against her mocha skin and long locks of curly dark hair. She said, "This is Marge's first vacation in who knows how long. She's a little bit nervous to leave all her babies alone with me."

I said, "Vacation? Where are you going?"

Marge tilted her head. "Well, if I had a brain cell left I'd take all that money and go down to the Bahamas for a month or twelve, but instead I'm renting a truck and driving over to my sister's place in Pensacola. There's a big estate auction nearby, so I'm bringing back all kinds of new furniture for the cats. And also . . ." She hesitated slightly. "I'm headed for New Orleans."

"You're kidding me."

She said, "I'm not. Guidry's wedding is tomorrow."

I took a deep breath and sat down on the carpet next to Franklin. "Yeah. So I've heard."

Marge said, "Dixie, I'm sorry. I should have mentioned it before, but I didn't think you'd want to hear it. Guidry's mother and my mother are friends, and my sister went to college with him, so she's going too, and it's only an hour or so from her house, so I figured, why not?"

I tried to regain my composure. "Oh, please. I don't care. I was planning on going myself, but I had to cancel at the last minute."

"I'm sure it must be a little strange for you . . ."

"Honestly, it's no big deal." I gave Franklin a couple of long strokes down his back and tried to change the subject. "I'm pretty sure this fella's house is still classified as an active crime scene, but as soon as they're done I can take him back home. I'm hoping maybe by tomorrow."

Franklin nuzzled up against my knee.

Marge smiled. "I do believe he's glad to see you."

"I wanted to stop by earlier, but things have been a little crazy." I slipped my backpack off my shoulder and opened it up. "And then there's this . . ."

Marge peered inside and gasped. "Oh my gosh. Is that a rabbit?"

"It is. He's Franklin's housemate." I gave her as charming a smile as I could muster. "I know he's not exactly your usual clientele, but I was wondering . . ."

"Well, of course! We had rabbits when I was little." She lowered her voice to a whisper. "My daddy bred them for meat, but I promise he's safe with me."

"His name's Gigi. I'm worried he might be getting a little tired of riding around on my back."

She lifted him out and nuzzled him to her chest, cooing softly. "Well, hello there, Mr. Gigi. Welcome to the Haven!"

If Marge thought the name Gigi was unusual for a boy, she kept it to herself. Over the years, she's helped me with all kinds of animals that needed safe harbor from a troubled home, and she's welcomed each and every one of them with open arms. Even Jaz was a bit of a troubled stray when I first introduced them, but Marge took Jaz under her wing with no questions asked. All she cares about is the here and now—a true believer in life, liberty, and the pursuit of treats—and she has zero interest in people's pasts, no matter how sordid or complicated. As I made my way out to the Bronco, I made a mental note to tell my brother that if he and Paco ever get tired of taking care of me, they should just drop me off at the Kitty Haven.

I found Deputy Morgan slouched down in his seat with the newspaper draped over the steering wheel. I was about to rap on the top of the hood to wake him when he sat up and said, "Where to now, boss?"

I said, "Ever hear of the Scarlet Woman of Siesta Key?"

21

As soon as I turned down Old Vineyard Lane, my heart felt just the tiniest bit lighter. I had expected the front of Caroline's house to be littered with evidence markers, sheriff's cruisers, and police tape, but there was just a lone crime cleanup van parked in the driveway, which meant I might be able to get Franklin and Gigi home sooner than I thought.

"Hey, good news for bunnies!"

My backpack was open on the passenger seat next to me, and I almost reached inside to give Gigi a scratch before I remembered he wasn't there. Now I understood why Caroline liked having him around so much. Life is better with a furry friend in tow—no doubt about it.

Next door, the front of Elba Kramer's house was hidden from the street by a looming hedge, and across the driveway's entrance was a tall wrought-iron gate with menacing spikes. There was an intercom pad on a stone pedestal to the left, and just as I was about to roll down my window, I heard two short beeps and the gate swung open. I pulled up and parked in the shade of a giant jacaranda tree as the gate closed behind me.

The landscaping around the house was so perfect it seemed almost artificial. The lush shrubs were all straight lines and right angles, and the thick grass was a flawless emerald green and perfectly manicured. Just then I noticed a woman in a wide-brimmed hat, long black slacks, and a white, long-sleeved blouse at the far side of the yard. She was reaching into the hedge and pulling out individual leaves, which she dropped into a metal bucket at her feet.

I was about to call to her when the front door of the house swung open, and out stepped a woman in a pair of sheer white linen slacks and a low-cut gauzy blouse. She had long dark hair that flowed past her shoulders, with a necklace of chunky turquoise stones hanging around her neck.

I gasped. By then I'd probably seen about a hundred pictures of Elba Kramer, but in person her beauty was astonishing, made all the more surprising by the fact that by conventional standards, she was—there's no other way to put it—downright ugly. Her eyes were too widely set, her lips off-kilter, and her nose, although narrow, had a decidedly pronounced bump in the middle. It looked awkward and out of place, as if it might have been more at home on the face of a hockey player or a professional boxer. Still, somehow, everything came together as seamlessly as a Picasso: honest, vibrant, and above all, alluring. I could see why a man might be tempted to risk his entire career for her.

That morning all those years ago, when I'd responded to what I thought was just another routine public-disturbance call only to find an enraged, half-naked senator screaming at some tourists, Ms. Kramer had already hidden herself down in the lower level of the yacht. I never talked to her, and if she'd seen me at all it would have been from a pretty good distance, so I didn't think she'd ever recognize me. But now, when she held out her hand to shake mine, I saw a flash of something in her eyes . . . a distant glint of recognition.

"Hello, Dixie. I'm Elba Kramer. Welcome to Custom House."

She stepped back to reveal a wide hallway with dark polished floors and a half-dozen crystal chandeliers hung across the vaulted ceiling. Down the center of the hall was a plush red carpet, and as she motioned me in, I noticed it had been newly vacuumed.

"Please."

I walked ahead, conscious of her eyes on my back. Midway down the hall were two doors on either side—one closed, but the door on the left was standing open. Ms. Kramer stepped around me and smiled.

She said, "We can talk in the living room. I'll open the windows and let some fresh air in."

I was about to follow when she stopped abruptly in the doorway and I almost bumped into her. It was a small, dark room. The one wall I could see was covered from floor to ceiling with shelves of leather-bound books.

On the floor was an intricately woven Persian rug with a giant antique desk in the middle, on top of which were about five cardboard boxes, each with labels in various languages. A few read FRAGILE.

The first thing I thought was that the room stuck out from the rest of the house like a sore thumb—completely out of sync with the light, modern decor everywhere else. It was fusty and crowded, so much so that if I had looked away one second earlier I wouldn't have noticed the elderly man that was slumped in a leather armchair behind the desk. He was jowly faced, with thinning red hair raked over his head and an unlit cigar dangling from his fat lips. He held a remote control in one hand, which he was pointing at an old, boxy television like he was holding it hostage. There was a somber-looking newscaster talking about oil prices as a ticker of stock market figures rolled across the bottom of the screen.

Ms. Kramer laid her hand on the doorknob and pulled it toward us, blocking my view.

She said, "Everything okay, Al?"

There was an indecipherable grunt from inside.

"Albert's not feeling very social today." She turned and whispered as she shut the door behind her. "Or *ever.*"

I smiled to myself. His name fit him perfectly. I could hear my grandmother's voice: *That man is such an Albert!* Paco had said Ms. Kramer and her husband owned an expensive women's accessories store in the Village, but Albert hardly seemed like the kind of man to trifle with jewelry and fancy women's things. I knew the type well— gruff and inelegant, perpetually in a bad mood. There'd been a lot of them on the force, although that rough exterior was usually just a cover-up for a sweeter version hidden inside. I had a feeling Albert reserved that part of himself for Elba Kramer alone.

She continued ahead, her stride long and confident, tempered only by a slightly restless fluttering of her hands. "He only comes out of his study to eat. It's just work, work, work. My sweet Jane has her cage, and he has his!"

The hallway opened into a sprawling living area. To the right was a full bar, glistening with hundreds of cocktail glasses of all shapes and sizes, and to the left was a giant marble fireplace big enough to park a car in. There was a sunken area in the middle of the room, with a trio of low-backed couches circling a marble-topped coffee table and a giant glass bowl piled high with lemons and grapefruit. It was all pretty breathtaking, but the most notable feature of the room, and the most impressive, was the back wall. It was made entirely of glass, and the view was nothing short of spectacular. I could see the entire span of the John Ringling Bridge sparkling over the bay, and I could even see halfway down the western shoreline of Siesta Key.

Before I could say a word, Ms. Kramer nonchalantly pressed a button next to the fireplace, and I watched in mute amazement as the entire glass wall lowered seamlessly into the floor.

Ms. Kramer said, "Fancy, huh?"

I managed a nod and a muffled, "Wow."

A rush of warm air moved in, and now it seemed as if we were sitting in a very nicely furnished outdoor patio, where the polished granite floor of the living room continued out to the covered patio, ending at a row of giant columns entwined in blooming mandevilla.

Rajinder appeared through a swinging door with a silver tray and two glasses of iced tea, each with a thinly sliced lemon wedge perched on the rim. He put the tray down on the coffee table, nodded discreetly, and then headed for the front hall. I noticed he was wearing woven grass slippers. They made a soft *shushing* sound as they slid along the tile floor.

Ms. Kramer stiffened. "Raji? What are you doing?"

He stopped and turned. "Mr. Kramer asked me to help him unpack the shipment that just arrived."

She shook her head. "No. I'll help him with it later. I need you to pick up that prescription now." She glanced at her watch. "I told you already. The pharmacy closes at six. If you don't leave now, you'll miss it."

Rajinder shrugged, which gave me the impression he didn't care one way or the other, either that or he was well accustomed to following Elba Kramer's every command. As he came back up the hall, Ms. Kramer sat down and handed me one of the glasses of iced tea.

"It's mint. From the garden. I'd like to take credit, but it's the gardener's doing. She's the one with the green thumb in this family, such as it is."

So far, Ms. Kramer hadn't mentioned why she needed me, like where she was going or for how long, nor had I seen any signs of a bird—which was, after all, the entire reason I was here—but I figured it must have been in a cage somewhere. Lots of bird owners give their feathered friends free reign of the house, but considering the entire back wall of Elba's living room was open to the outside, I doubted she'd let hers loose.

"Raji tells me you're perfectly qualified to care for my little girl, and Raji's a good judge of character. I'd trust him with my life, but I wanted to meet you first. This town's full of hacks looking for gossip to sell to the tabloids, and I've been fooled more than once. As you can imagine, I have to be very careful about who I let in my house."

I nodded self-consciously, wondering what was the proper etiquette for meeting a semicelebrity. Was it more polite to acknowledge that, yes, I knew all about her exploits in the tabloids, or was it better to be discreet and treat her like any other client? And would she be offended, or even suspicious, if I pretended I'd never heard of her?

She smiled. "I've seen that look before. It's fine. I get a good vibe from you."

I cleared my throat, realizing I'd barely said a word since I'd arrived. I said, "Ms. Kramer, I take my job very seriously, and I treat all my clients with the same degree of professionalism, no matter who they are. I would never in a million years reveal any personal details about you to anyone, least of all the press."

"That's good to know." She set her glass down on the table as her expression darkened. "So . . . shall we discuss the elephant in the room?"

My heart skipped a beat.

The "elephant in the room" could only mean one thing—I was right. She *had* recognized me. It also suddenly dawned on me that even if she hadn't immediately recognized my name, the chances she'd run a background check before deciding to hire me were very high. In fact, I wouldn't have been a bit surprised if she knew every bit as much about my past as I did about hers . . . which meant she was probably well aware that our paths had crossed once before. And now I was in the very awkward situation of explaining why I hadn't owned up to it earlier.

I said, "Ms. Kramer, first of all, I'm sorry I didn't say something when we first talked on the phone. But you have to understand, I was just doing my job. There's a very strict code of ethics when it comes to law enforcement, and even though I'm a pet sitter now, I still have to be very careful not to violate anyone's rights under the law, no matter how long it's been, even if I'm talking to someone . . ." I gestured in her direction, trying to come up with the right words. "You know, someone who was . . . *involved*."

"Involved! What makes you think I was involved?" She shook her head and snorted. "Oh, my god. What a stupid cow!"

My chin dropped and I felt my hands curl into fists. Yes, that business on the boat had eventually led to the end of Senator Cobb's political career, and it had definitely put another black mark on Elba Kramer's reputation, so I could understand why she might be angry—even though in the end it certainly wasn't all my fault. It wasn't as if she hadn't put a few black marks there herself. But if this was the tone she was going to take, there was no point in my hanging around. I was in no mood for this woman's drama. I'd had a hard enough week as it was.

I stood up and pulled my backpack over my shoulder. "Okay. Again, I apologize. If you'd like me to give you recommendations for other pet sitters, I'd be happy to do that, but this is obviously not going to work out."

She shot off the sofa and made a step toward the front door, as if she might try to stop me. "Wait a minute. At least tell me what she's saying!"

"Huh?"

She shook her head, disgust plainly visible on her face. "This is absolutely unbelievable. I should have known. When those cops came over here all full of questions, acting all suspicious . . . there's no telling what that stupid woman has told them about me."

I said, "Hold on. Who are we talking about?"

"Caroline Greaver! Who else? No wonder that detective acted so damn weird. The woman could barely look me in the eye."

I said, "Wait . . ." But she continued, getting more and more agitated.

"Listen, whatever you've been told about me, it's complete baloney. I mean, yes, it's no secret Caroline and I are not exactly the best of friends, but this is low even for her. And you can be damn sure of one thing: if I ever got myself involved in a murder, Caroline Greaver would *not* be around to talk about it after!"

I said, "Oh, no. Ms. Kramer, there's been a misunderstanding. I wasn't talking about the murder. And Caroline hasn't said a thing about you as far as I know."

She put her hands on her hips. "Then what did you

mean by all that stuff about me being *involved,* and your strict code of ethics?"

I said, "Wow. I feel like an idiot. When you said the 'elephant' in the room, I thought you meant . . ." I took a deep breath and sighed. "Ms. Kramer, I didn't say anything before because I didn't think it mattered, and also I didn't want to embarrass you, but . . . long before I became a pet sitter, I was a sheriff's deputy."

She shook her head impatiently. "So . . . ?"

"So, I was the officer that was called to the scene that day . . ."

"What scene?"

"Um . . . the scene when you were caught with Senator Cobb . . . on his yacht."

Her eyes widened. "That was *you?*"

I nodded.

Her jaw opened slightly and then she threw her head back and burst into laughter.

I stammered. "I'm sorry. I just didn't want to embarrass you."

She fell back down on the couch and held both hands up in the air. "Thank you! Finally something interesting in this godforsaken town! Honey, the elephant in the room I was talking about was that horrible business next door, not Morton Cobb!" She reached for a cocktail napkin from the tray and unfolded it. "I've always wondered what happened to you. Morton swore up and down he'd have you fired for not confiscating those tourists' cameras, and now . . . Oh gosh, I suppose that's what happened isn't it? Is that why you're no longer a deputy?"

I sat back down on the couch. "No. Although he did

threaten me that day, that's for sure. But I quit the force years ago . . . for personal reasons. It was totally unrelated."

She sighed, wiping tears of laughter from her eyes with the corner of a napkin. "That man is completely insane, you know. He's still snooping around trying to get back at me somehow. He had it in his head he'd be *president* one day. Can you believe that? I guess the world has *you* to thank for putting a stop to that. It's funny, when Raji first mentioned your name, I did think it sounded vaguely familiar. I just couldn't put my finger on it."

I said, "Well, I've always felt bad, but there really was nothing I could do. Those tourists hadn't done anything illegal."

"Oh, please. We were lucky you didn't arrest us both for public indecency. And, anyway, the whole episode gave me an excuse to leave him. And my God! How bizarre that you're here now, especially with everything that's happened next door!"

I sat up, remembering the crime cleanup crew. "You know, I should probably meet your bird before it gets too late. I'm hoping I can bring Caroline's pets back home, maybe even tonight. I think the police might be finishing up their investigation. And also, your assistant mentioned something about a nondisclosure agreement?"

She rolled her eyes. "Oh, good grief. That's Albert's doing. He always expects the worst in everyone, but I could care less. And, anyway, my life is an open book. Always has been. He'll probably ask you to sign one, though. I hope that's not a problem."

I shook my head. "Of course not."

"Good." She glanced at her watch. "Let's go over to the pool house."

I took my backpack and followed her through the living room out to the pool, which was a deep indigo blue in the failing light. On the far side were three red umbrellas hovering over a line of white lounge chairs, each perfectly parallel to one another, and beyond that was a low-slung building, almost like a tiki hut or a cabana but bigger and fancier, with three sets of folding glass doors and matching red curtains held open with white cords. I couldn't see it, but somewhere nearby a fountain was gurgling.

"Oh, wow," I said. "This is beautiful."

Ms. Kramer winked. "I know. Having a rich husband does have its perks."

I grinned. "Ha. I wouldn't know."

She held her arm out and looked at her watch again, which she'd done so many times I was beginning to think she needed to be somewhere, but now that I had a closer look, I realized her motive was a little simpler: she was showing off.

It hardly looked like a watch at all—more like an elegant gold bracelet with an oval-shaped bauble in the center. Only this was no ordinary bauble. It was a platinum gold watch face, encrusted with so many diamonds that even in the fading twilight it gleamed and glittered impressively.

Ms. Kramer smiled. "You should definitely try it. I recommend everyone have at least one rich husband before they die."

The living area inside the pool house was just as spacious and exquisitely decorated as the main residence, with the same polished granite flooring and sleek, modern furniture, including a white leather sofa and two red velvet armchairs around a long rectangular glass coffee table. Ms. Kramer pointed down a hallway just beyond the kitchen.

"The guest room is down there, and then beyond that is the spa. It's divine. You're welcome to use it while you're here. There's a hot tub and a steam room, and beyond that are two showers and then a dry sauna. None of this was here when I met Al, just the pool. It was the first thing I did after we got married. I literally could not face the world without a steam room. Do you know what I mean?"

I gave her a half nod, followed by a quick shake of the head. "Actually, no. I've never been in a steam room in my life."

She turned, her face suddenly somber. "What? You've got to be kidding."

"No. Never."

She shook her head. "Okay, that's literally the saddest thing I've ever heard."

I was beginning to wonder what in the world we were doing out here, mostly because I didn't see a bird anywhere, nor, for that matter, did I hear one. It suddenly dawned on me that perhaps Ms. Kramer was expecting me to stay at her house while she was away.

I said, "You know, I don't normally do overnight visits, although we could arrange it, but generally I charge more for . . ."

Her face changed slightly, a subtle narrowing of her eyes, but enough to make me stop talking, and then I heard a sound, almost like a muffled typewriter, but louder somehow—*Pop pop pop pop pop pop!*

Ms. Kramer frowned slightly. "What the hell was that?"

I'd heard that sound only once before, but it had stayed with me for more than a decade. During my training for the force, a deputy from the Miami sheriff's department had given a presentation on how rapidly changing technology presents an ongoing challenge to law enforcement officers. If I was right, the sound we had just heard was an automatic rifle with a high-tech silencer attached.

Ms. Kramer took one step toward the living room with a puzzled look on her face. "It sounded like it came from the house."

Just then, a man's voice broke through the silence. He shouted something, but I couldn't tell what, and then there were two more gunshots, much louder this time. As Ms. Kramer and I looked at each other, the sound of tires screeching on pavement came from somewhere beyond the house, and then we heard the grinding of a car's engine recede into the distance.

Ms. Kramer whispered, "Albert . . ."

I reached for her wrist, but it was too late.

She ran.

22

As Elba Kramer rushed out of the pool house, I didn't move. I just stood there, my feet glued to the floor. The sound we'd heard was gunfire—of that I was certain. A siren had started up in the distance, just barely audible over the chirruping of the crickets, so it was hard to tell exactly how far away it was—or from what direction—but I figured south, probably taking the longer but faster route up Midnight Pass to avoid Ocean Boulevard traffic.

I told myself to breathe. Blood was coursing through my body harder than I thought possible—I could feel it behind my eyes and in the tips of my fingers—and there was a loud banging in my ears, like a bass drum pounding to the beat of my heart.

I cursed myself for being so stupid. The moment there'd been even the slightest hint that someone was after me, I should have listened to Detective Carthage. I should have stayed home. I should have called each and every one of my clients and told them I'd have to send someone else to look after their pets until this whole thing was over.

I took a couple of feeble steps forward, but apparently the lecture I'd given myself about no longer moving through life with fear hadn't quite yet taken effect. Every muscle in my body was telling me to turn around and run like hell in the opposite direction.

But I knew I couldn't.

I reached into the side compartment of my backpack for my pistol, which seemed ridiculously small now given the circumstances, but I pulled it out anyway and released the safety. Then I willed myself forward, walking on rubbery legs through the pool house and out to the patio, all the while keeping my gun steady and my eyes open for any sign of movement.

It was eerily quiet.

I followed the edge of the pool and then slid in behind one of the columns by the back porch, feeling the vines brush the back of my neck. I had a feeling I knew what those louder shots had been shortly after the rapid gunfire: Deputy Morgan's pistol. He'd followed me here, and I knew he was still outside. I just couldn't remember if he'd driven through the gate when I arrived or if he had parked in the street.

A chill ran down my spine. I had just assumed the gunfire had come from inside the house, but it dawned on me now that it could just as easily have come from *outside*—from the driveway or beyond the front gate in the street. In which case, Morgan . . .

I shook my head.

No. I told myself not to panic, to try to concentrate

and focus on one thing at a time, and for now the only thing I needed to do was find Ms. Kramer.

I peered around the column through the vines. I could see into the living room, but there was no one there. I leaned out a little farther to get a view down the long hall to the front door, but still there was nothing. Just as I was about to make a move, a gut-wrenching scream—high-pitched and piercing—echoed through the house.

I moved out from behind the column just in time to see a shadow fall across the open door of Mr. Kramer's study, and then Ms. Kramer stepped into the hallway, cradling something in her arms. She was staring at the open door of the room on the opposite side of the hall, her back erect, her chin tipped up slightly.

Almost at the exact same moment, the front door burst open to reveal Deputy Morgan with his gun drawn. There was a look of sheer panic on his face. He shouted, "Is everybody okay?"

I said, "We're fine, but Ms. Kramer's husband . . ."

"Where is he?"

I pointed at the study.

Elba Kramer had barely moved. She was still staring straight ahead, unblinking and barely acknowledging Morgan's presence.

He said, "Ms. Kramer, I'm Deputy Jesse Morgan with the Sarasota Sheriff's Department. Is your husband okay?"

There was a pause, and then she turned in my direction without answering. Whatever she'd seen inside that study had thrown her into a complete state of shock.

Morgan took a couple of steps toward the door and

looked inside. His face went pale. He held up one hand as he unclipped his radio. "You better take her outside."

Ms. Kramer was moving toward me like a sleep-walker, her face an empty mask, her eyes wide open and distant, and now I could see what she was holding in her arms. It was a domed birdcage about the size of a lampshade. Inside was a small bird, although it was flinging around the cage so fast all I could see was a yellow blur. I stepped aside as Ms. Kramer came closer. I thought I heard the bird twittering, but then realized the sound was coming from Ms. Kramer. She was talk-ing to herself, like a whimpering child.

"I should have known. We should have left this god-forsaken place years ago . . . we could've gone *anywhere*." Her eyes glassed over when she looked at me. "I tried to tell him. We could have gone anywhere, anywhere in the world. France or Mexico, anywhere we wanted. We could have gotten away . . ."

She continued out to the patio, and when the cage hit the light, it gleamed and sparkled. I remember think-ing it had to be gold-plated, or maybe even solid 14-carat. I glanced at Morgan, who was still standing in the door-way. There was a trail of small yellow feathers sprinkled along the red carpet where Ms. Kramer had walked.

I said, "What happened?"

He said, "I was parked in front of the house. I heard gunfire and ran up as fast as I could. The front window was blown to bits and there was a man running around the side of the house with a rifle. I fired, but I don't know if I hit him or not. I was climbing over the gate when I heard a car speed off."

I said, "Ms. Kramer's husband . . ."

He shook his head. "You don't want to see it. The whole room's been sprayed with bullets. They shot right through the curtains."

And then it hit me: the heady, sweet smell of magnolia that had permeated the air in my driveway. Instantly, the image of Mrs. Reed's body flashed in my mind. I bent over and put my hands on my knees. I was having some kind of hallucinatory flashback, imagining the overpowering scent of those flowers. It seemed so real I could actually taste it in my mouth.

I said, "I need some air."

I went through the living room and out to the pool, where Elba was sitting on one of the lounge chairs in front of the pool house, slumped over the gold birdcage in her lap. For a split second, I thought the cage was empty, but then I saw the small bird sitting still on the cage floor. It was banana-yellow, with an orange beak and small eyes like black ink spots. It looked absolutely terrified, as if it had just been through the most horrific ordeal imaginable, which of course it had. It was a miracle it was still alive.

Ms. Kramer had a cold, distant expression on her face, but there were tears streaming down her cheeks. When she sensed my presence, she looked up, and even from several feet away I could see that her eyes were completely swollen and bloodshot.

She said, "He's dead, right?"

I always say our local law enforcement has some of the best officers in the business, but even I was impressed with how quickly they arrived on the scene. Someone must have called 911 the moment that gunfire rang out, because by the time I made my way along the side of the house to the front, there were at least a half-dozen emergency vehicles surrounding the place, with all kinds of sheriff's deputies and Sarasota policemen, as well as two guys in suits walking around looking official and flashing their badges at everyone in sight.

Detective Carthage had arrived shortly after. I waited behind some bushes until one of the deputies led him into the house where Ms. Kramer was waiting, and then I walked right across the lawn, trying to look as cool and calm as possible, which must have worked because no one seemed to notice me. I might as well have been a ghost.

When I got to the Bronco, I didn't even look around. I got behind the wheel and shut the door as quietly as possible, then I closed my eyes and sat there for a good minute or so, watching the muted colors of the emergency lights as they played across the insides of my eyelids. I concentrated on willing whatever part of my brain was creating the smell of those magnolia blossoms to stop. Gradually, it faded—which was a good thing, because otherwise I would've thought I'd finally lost my mind.

The giant front gate was standing open, but I knew any minute they'd be stringing up police tape, so I started up the engine, sunk down in my seat, and rolled out the driveway. At the corner, I turned right and headed for Ocean Boulevard.

Third time's a charm, the note had said.

Apparently not, I thought . . .
I'm still alive.

The whole way home, I felt surprisingly calm, despite the fact—or maybe because of it—that my brain was filled with blank noise, like a chalkboard that's been written over so many times it's turned completely white.

At some point, my cell phone rang but I didn't bother to see who it was. Instead, I plugged it into the car charger and switched the ringer off, and then I focused on the road in the glow of the Bronco's headlights. About a mile or so outside the village, something small darted into the bushes on my left—a squirrel or a rabbit—and I thought of Franklin and Gigi.

They were still waiting at the Kitty Haven. I figured I'd have to ask Ethan to go and check on them, and maybe even take them home when the investigators were done with Caroline's house—although given what had just happened next door, I imagined that could very well be delayed even longer. Practically all of Old Vineyard Lane was an active crime scene now.

Long before I got to my house, I pulled over on the right, making sure there were no headlights coming in either direction, and then rolled into a sandy clearing, hidden from the road by a stand of scrubby pines and chest-high beach grass. Luckily, the moon had risen above the treetops, so I was able to make my way without much trouble. I followed a narrow trail through the brush down to the beach and then walked the rest of the way along the water's edge. When I was about a hundred yards from the house, I sat down on an old overturned skiff that was tethered to a rusty pole stuck in the sand. It'd been there for as long as I could remember. When we were kids, Michael and I would paddle around in it, pretending we were marauding pirates, but to this day I have no idea who it belongs to. Probably no one.

I pulled out my cell phone. There were seven missed calls from Detective Carthage.

Ethan answered on the first ring.

"Dixie, the cops just called. Where are you?"

Keeping my voice to a whisper, I said, "I'm just down the beach from the house. Where are you?"

"I'm working late, but—"

I said, "Okay, listen, we need to talk."

"You're damn right we need to talk! The detective told me you just disappeared. What were you thinking?"

I said, "Okay, did he tell you what else happened?"

There was a pause. "Look, just stay where you are. I'll be there in ten minutes, and we can figure it out."

"No." I shook my head. "There's nothing to figure out. Somebody's after me. They want to kill me, or terrify me, or just plain kill everybody around me. Either way, I can't risk you or anybody else getting hurt too. I need to get as far away from here as possible."

"Dixie, are you crazy? Just wait for me."

"Ethan, no. I'll be gone before you get here. It's not safe. Promise me you won't come."

There was a long pause. "Okay. I promise."

"And you have to get ahold of Michael and Paco and

tell them everything. I don't think it's safe for anybody here."

There was silence.

I said, "Did you hear me?"

"Yes, I'll call them right now . . . but I don't like this one bit."

I said, "Me neither. You just have to trust I know what I'm doing."

"Okay, I trust you. I really do. But where are you gonna go?"

"I don't know, but I'll call you when I get there."

Before he could say another word, I snapped the phone shut and cringed. I hated hanging up on him, but he was right. I had no idea where I could go that was safe. All I knew was that whatever maniac was on my trail seemed to be constantly one step ahead. They'd known where I lived. They'd known I would be at Caroline's house. They'd known I had an appointment with Elba Kramer.

But how?

I was still sitting on the edge of the boat in the dark, holding my cell phone. It was one of those old flip types, ancient by today's standards. Ethan and Michael and Paco had been teasing me about it for years, but I'd stubbornly refused to exchange it for a more modern model, not only because I'm a dyed-in-the-wool Luddite when it comes to technology but also because it had originally belonged to Todd. I liked having it.

I looked down and turned it over a couple of times in my hand.

Was it possible someone was tracking my phone's GPS signal? Were they using my phone to monitor my movement around the island? Or had they somehow listened in on my calls? I'd have thought that kind of thing would require some pretty sophisticated technical skills, or at least inside access to the phone company's servers, but hacking is not exactly my field of expertise. For all I knew, anybody with half a brain and a fourth-grade education could pull it off.

I glanced up at the darkened ocean, its gentle waves twinkling in the moonlight like a field of fireflies.

"Huh."

I stood up and flipped the boat over. The inside was covered in rust and filled with old cobwebs. Lashed to the seat was an old wooden oar that looked like it might fall apart if you touched it. In fact, I wondered if the whole boat wouldn't break into pieces and sink the moment I put it in the water.

Well, I thought as I kicked off my shoes. *There's only one way to find out.*

I dragged it across the sand into the surf until the waves were lapping at my knees and the boat was gently swaying up and down. Miraculously, it seemed more or less seaworthy. I untied the oar and used the frayed rope to secure my phone to the seat deck as snugly as possible—I didn't want it to get thrown overboard if the waves got too rough—and then, without even the slightest nod to what surely would feel like a ceremonious occasion later, I gave the boat a good shove.

All the way to the house, I watched over my shoulder as the waves gently ferried it out into the darkness.

23

I t's strange . . .

I don't consider myself to be particularly plugged into the modern world. I still have a rotary phone on my desk along with one of those old digital answering machines. I don't have a Facebook account or, for that matter, a computer (shocking, I know), and I don't tweet, poke, like, or click . . . *ever*. I'm totally fine with it. But as I made my way down the beach in the dark, with Todd's old cell phone drifting out to sea behind me, I felt completely, thoroughly, *inevitably* . . . alone.

It wasn't an altogether unpleasant feeling, though. In fact, for the first time in days, I felt like I was in complete control of my own world. If it was true that somebody was tracking my cell phone's position, they'd think I was headed out into the Gulf right now, drifting to Mexico or Texas or wherever the waves wanted to carry that boat. Of course, it was entirely possible they'd carry the damn thing right back to shore, but I tried not to think about that. At least now I had time to make a plan.

I hadn't wanted to leave a trail leading away from my launching point, so I stayed knee-deep in the water, about a yard out from the edge, shuffling my feet in the sand to ward off stingrays and praying there were no jellyfish floating around. When I got even with the house, I walked backward out of the water until I reached the dunes, slipped my shoes back on, and then snuck through the woods. At the edge of the courtyard, I crouched down behind an old coco-plum bush and waited.

Everything was still.

I knew Michael wouldn't be home—his shift at the firehouse had started that afternoon—but I couldn't be so sure about Paco. His schedule is always a mystery, so there was no way of knowing if he was at work or not. I could see a single light glowing in the kitchen window of the main house, which was definitely a good sign, but I'd have to check the carport to know for sure.

After a few minutes, my eyes started to sting, and I realized I was scanning the darkness so intently I'd forgotten to blink. If anybody was there—hiding in the shadows and waiting for me to come home—they were doing a damn good job of it. I decided I'd just have to trust my gut, which was telling me there was no one here . . . yet.

I tiptoed around the edge of the deck and paused at the kitchen window. The only light came from the exhaust hood over the stove. Ella was curled up in one of the bar stools at the center island, sleeping soundly.

I let out a sigh of relief. That was the best proof I could hope for that no one else was here. I knew Ella would've run for cover if a stranger had showed up.

Thank God for small favors, I thought.

As I climbed the steps to my apartment, doing my best to avoid the squeaky spots, I shook my head. Here I was, sneaking around like a lunatic, convinced I was being followed by a serial killer and sensing danger at every turn. And yet, given the circumstances, what choice did I have?

When I opened the door, I silently thanked Ethan for locking it when he left for work. At least I didn't have to worry about somebody jumping out from under my bed with a machine gun. Even so, I could feel my heart pounding in my chest. There was something eerily un-settling about creeping through my living room in the middle of the night . . . like a burglar in my own home.

The hallway was darker, so dark in fact that I had to feel my away along the walls to the closet, where I slid my fingers across the desk until they bumped into the cold brass base of the lamp. I didn't dare turn it on, but just next to it was a candle and a box of matches—a rem-nant of the time when our electricity could go out at the drop of a coconut. These days it's a lot more dependable, but I still keep a candle in every room just in case.

As soon as I struck the match, the whole closet filled with ghoulish shadows, but I ignored them. I slid the door shut so the light wouldn't show down the hall, and then I pulled out my suitcase and threw some clothes in, barely paying attention to what I was grabbing. The entire time, I had the weirdest feeling I was being watched, but I ignored that too.

When I was done, I went over to the desk and picked up the phone. I figured I couldn't just run off without calling Michael. He'd never forgive me for not at least giving him a chance to talk me out of it.

As soon as I heard his voice, I knew he'd already talked to Ethan. He didn't even say hello when he answered. His voice had that authoritative, *older-brother* edge to it.

"Dixie, what's happening?"

"I'm fine. Just a little shaken up."

"I've called your cell phone a hundred times."

I said, "I know, but listen: I was at Elba Kramer's tonight, and somebody shot the place up with an automatic rifle. They killed her husband."

"I know. I talked to Ethan, and Detective Carthage called looking for you too. He said you just drove off . . . ?"

"I didn't know what else to do. I mean, that makes three people killed. And that note left on Edith Reed's body said, 'Third time's a charm.'"

"Yeah?"

"So, don't you see? Somebody knew I was there, and I think they just assumed we were in the front room because that's where Elba keeps her bird. Michael, they meant to kill *me*."

"Dixie, I'm sure there's an explanation for all of this . . ."

"Well, if there is, I'm not waiting around to find out. If somebody wants to murder me, they're gonna have to find me first."

Michael said, "Okay, listen. I asked Detective Carthage about that. He said they can keep you safe until this whole thing blows over."

"Right. In a holding cell at the station. No, thank you.

And anyway, I'm not putting anybody else in danger again. If whoever's after me found out I was there, who's to say they wouldn't walk in with a machine gun and mow the whole sheriff's office down?" There was a long pause. I said, "Look, Michael, I'll be fine. I made sure nobody followed me."

"Dixie, there's no way in hell I'm letting you drive off in the middle of the night by yourself. First of all, where will you go?"

For a split second, I considered the possibility that the house phone might have been tapped, which was probably as good an indication as any that I'd turned into a complete, paranoid mess. But I wasn't taking any chances.

I said, "I don't know. I'm just gonna . . . drift."

He said, "Okay, I've got an idea. Come to the firehouse. One of the guys here has a fishing cabin at Lake Parrish. I'm sure he'll let us use it. Come get me and we'll drive up there together. They can send a deputy to go with us. We can stay there until they catch whoever this maniac is."

I thought for a second. A remote fishing cabin in the backwood swamps of Florida sounded exactly like the kind of place I'd want to be if I was being stalked by a crazed serial killer. I said, "Okay. But Michael, you have to promise me you'll stay put until I get there."

There was a pause. "Of course . . ."

I said, "I'm on my way," and hung up.

As I passed the kitchen, I noticed the basket of mail on the counter, with Guidry's wedding invitation inside. There was a shaft of moonlight falling across it from the kitchen window, which made it float in the surrounding darkness, like a piece of space garbage lost in the infinite, unknowable universe.

Well, I thought to myself. *No time like the present!*

I tore the envelope open and pulled the card out.

Jean Pierre Guidry and Monica Alice Diderot request the honor of your presence at the Saint Louis Cathedral, New Orleans, to witness their union in the sacrament of holy matrimony. In lieu of gifts, the bride and groom request that donations be sent to the Children's Police Fund of New Orleans.

For a minute, I just stood there staring at the time and date. The wedding was tomorrow morning, which meant right now, while I was running around in the dark like a hunted animal, Guidry was probably sitting in a fancy restaurant or a chic, crowded bar, surrounded by friends and good cheer, drinking a toast to new beginnings, his buddies teasing him about his old ball-and-chain and saluting his last hours of freedom. I wondered what he would do if he knew what was happening to me . . .

Would he even care?

I shook my head. At that point, I think the lurking realization that I'd sent my cell phone, *Todd's* cell phone, floating out into the ocean had somehow unleashed all sorts of feelings in me . . . feelings I hadn't expected . . . feelings I had no idea what to do with. I dropped the invitation back in the basket and headed for the door.

Luckily, not a single car went by as I lugged my suitcase along the roadside back to the Bronco, but as soon as I got in behind the wheel, two deputy cruisers roared by at top speed, one right after the other. I knew Detective Carthage wouldn't be too happy, considering I'd left the scene of a crime without letting him question me first, but I also knew he wouldn't want me left alone for one more second. I just hoped Michael or Ethan would explain to him why I was running away. It was for everyone's own good that I disappear . . . the problem was, where could I disappear to?

As much as I wanted to, I didn't dare meet Michael at the fire station. His intentions were good, but I know him all too well. There was no way he meant to take me to some cabin in the woods. I knew beyond a shadow of a doubt he'd be there waiting for me, along with Paco and Detective Carthage and probably a couple of deputies to accompany me to a holding pen at the sheriff's department.

There was only one place I knew where no one would ever think to look for me . . .

24

There are all kinds of retirement homes and assisted-living communities in Sarasota, but Bayfront Village is the queen of them all, despite the fact that its exterior is a garish, Pepto-Bismol pink and its architecture is a mishmash of styles, with beet-red terra-cotta shingles on the roof, faux-gold Gothic spires rising from all the corners, and gaudy, turquoise tiles plastered along the roofline. But at night, with its banks of windows twinkling against the dark sky, it doesn't look much different from any of the other high-rise-condo buildings that stand in a gaggle at the edge of the bay. In front, there's a white wrought-iron gate that leads down a cobblestone drive to a Spanish-style portico, complete with cascading fountains and a couple of chubby concrete cherubs to herald your arrival.

My friend Cora lives on the sixth floor, and whenever my life starts to veer a little off course, I find myself floating to her. It's almost an unconscious instinct on my part, which is funny when you think about it, because she's practically three times my age. You'd think we wouldn't have much to talk about, but she's sharp as a tack, full of finely tuned wisdom, and she always leaves me feeling like my batteries have been one-hundred-percent rejuvenated.

I admit going to Cora's place wasn't the smartest move on my part, but I was so exhausted, and I just needed to be in the presence of something good . . . something honest. If only for a few moments.

I couldn't risk going in the front, though. I knew Vicki would be there, sitting at her concierge desk, and there are usually a couple of guards in the lobby and I didn't want to risk anybody recognizing me.

I parked behind the building and snuck through the manicured grounds, avoiding the pools of light from the gas lamps along the walkway. I knew there were at least three fire-escape doors in the back, each leading to emergency stairwells, so I was hoping maybe one of them might have been left open and I could slip in.

Just as I was about to try the handle of the first door, it opened and a thin woman in a black pencil skirt and pink blouse stepped out. I must have scared her as much as she scared me, because she jumped back a foot, dropping a lighter and a pack of cigarettes. We both knelt down to pick them up at the same time, and it was only then that I recognized her. It was Vicki, the concierge from the lobby.

She said, "Oh my gosh, Dixie, you scared me to death! What are you doing out here?"

I tried to think fast. "Oh, I was just taking a late night

stroll and . . . and then I thought I'd drop by, I mean, that's why I don't have a car. With me."

"Well, you caught me red-handed. This is strictly a no-smoking establishment, but it's been a long day, so . . ." She held up a cigarette and shrugged. "I didn't think anybody'd find me back here."

I mustered a smile. "Don't worry. I won't tell on you."

"I'll call up and let Cora know you're here. She's doing much better, by the way."

I frowned. "What do you mean *better*?"

Her eyes widened. "Oh, no. She swore up and down she'd already told you."

"Told me what?"

She sighed. "I shouldn't say anything, but you're practically family. There was an incident in the elevator on Tuesday. She fell. Luckily, one of the maintenance boys was there or it would have been much worse. She hit her head, and we were afraid she'd broken her hip, but it's fine. They gave her some pills for the pain, but you know Cora. She hates pills."

When I stepped off the elevator, Cora was waiting outside her apartment at the end of the hall. She's barely five feet, with knobby little knees, skinny arms, and hair as light and wispy as raw cotton. She grinned from ear to ear when she saw me, but even from a distance I could see a dark purple bruise hovering over her left eye, and she was holding herself up with two bright pink crutches.

She said, "Now, Dixie, before you say a word, I want

you to know that I'm perfectly fine. A little sore here and there, but believe me, it's not near as bad as it looks."

"Cora, what in the world happened?"

She gave me a kiss on the cheek. "I got *old* is what happened. I don't know how, but suddenly I'm an old lady."

I put my hands on my hips. "No offense, Cora, but you've been an old lady for as long as I've known you."

She grinned. "I know, dammit. Come on in and have some tea, and I'll tell you all about the great fall." She handed me the crutches. "Carry these."

"Wait. You don't need them?"

"They're supposed to take the weight off my hip, but they're just more trouble than they're worth. And the pills they gave me for the pain just knock me out cold."

She shuffled in ahead, even slower than usual, and once we were inside she said, "Lock that door behind you."

"Oh, no. I guess you saw the news, huh?"

She nodded grimly. "Three murders in one week. It's just terrible."

"Well, with all the staff downstairs, I think you're safe."

"Oh, it's not that. It's Reggie Anderson. He keeps dropping by unannounced."

"Reggie Anderson? Who's that?"

She flicked a hand in the air. "You might have seen him in the lobby. Lives on the third floor. Silver hair, handsome . . . once. He's sweet on me like syrup on a pancake."

I grinned. "You mean, he's your beau?"

"Beau? Such an old-fashioned word. *Now* who's the old lady? And no, for your information, he's not my beau, although I imagine that's exactly what he's got in his stupid bonehead. He's already stopped by two times today, and the last time he left *that* monstrosity."

She pointed at a vase of pink roses on the dining table.

I said, "Oh. He means business, doesn't he?"

"I don't know what to do about it."

"Well, what's so bad about a handsome man bringing you flowers?"

"Dixie, what's wrong is he's ten years older than me!"

I leaned her crutches against the small bar that separated the dining area from the kitchen. "Oh, come on. I'd think it'd be nice to have a man around the house. You know, to fix things."

Her eyes twinkled. "Dixie, trust me, what I've got is long past fixing."

"Okay, that's not what I meant!"

Just then a kettle whistled on the stove and Cora padded into the kitchen. I'd already prepared a bogus story to explain why I was showing up so late, but if Cora was curious about it, she didn't say a word. I leaned over the bar and watched her, hoping she had a loaf of her homemade chocolate bread in the works. She usually serves it warm, and when she slices into it, little rivers of chocolate ooze out and call my name.

There was no sign of the bread, though. She filled a teacup with steaming water and handed it to me. "And anyway, this is an assisted-living community. *Assisted!* That means there's a whole staff here that gets paid to fix stuff. What in the world do I need a man for?"

As I took a sip of tea, her eyes widened, almost as if she was seeing me for the first time.

"Oh, Dixie."

"What?"

"Sweetheart, you look exhausted."

I felt my eyes immediately well with tears. "I'm not surprised. I've had a . . ." I paused, searching for the right words.

"Bad day?"

I nodded. "More like a bad week."

"Oh, dear, and here I've been babbling on about my silly problems while you . . . Well, you look like you've been rode hard and hung up to dry. Why don't you go on in and lie down." She nodded toward the living room. "And drink that tea right up. It's delicious—elderberry, cinnamon, licorice root, plus a little secret ingredient of my own. It'll make you feel better right away."

I felt like a child being fussed over, but Cora was right. I *was* exhausted. And I knew if I stood there any longer, gazing into her clear blue eyes, so full of love and concern, I'd start crying like a baby. I did as I was told and ambled into the living room.

She was right about the tea too. It *was* delicious, with something vaguely sweet, yet spicy. I'd never tasted anything like it, but I knew right away it was exactly what the doctor ordered. I made a mental note to ask her what that secret ingredient was. I practically downed the whole cup by the time I got to the couch.

As soon as I laid down, my eyelids felt as heavy as a couple of sandbags. I could hear Cora fussing around in the kitchen, quietly talking to herself, or maybe humming some indecipherable song, one I thought maybe I'd heard before, and then I heard something low and rumbling in the background. I couldn't tell if it was coming from the kitchen, like an electric mixer or maybe (I hoped) a bread machine, but it didn't matter.

Within seconds, I was out like a light.

25

I knew he was there before I even opened my eyes.

I was on my side, curled up in a fetal position half buried in the overstuffed pillows on the couch, and right away I sensed it. A presence in the room. Something foreign. When I lifted my head, one of Cora's pillows toppled over the edge and landed on the floor. I reached out, feeling for it, and my hand touched what at first I thought was the leg of the coffee table.

I was wrong.

It was a man's knee. He was sitting in one of Cora's chintz armchairs next to the couch. Light was streaming in through the window behind him, so at first all I could make out was his trim, broad-shouldered silhouette. He was dressed in a dark suit and tie and had curly, unkempt hair. He had one long leg crossed over the other, his arms folded politely in his lap, and my first thought was that he must have been Cora's suitor. *What was his name? Reggie?*

The man tipped his chin and said, "Gid mornin', lass. Fancy a cuppa?"

That voice . . . I recognized it immediately. I squeezed my eyes shut and opened them again, but he was still there, watching me with a slightly bemused look in his eye.

It was Mr. Scotland.

"Have a nice kip, did we?"

I clenched my teeth. How could I have been so stupid? So naive? I'd gotten a weird feeling the moment I met him, and now here he was, sitting in Cora's apartment like he owned the place, watching me as I slept. I sat up slowly, my mind racing a mile a minute. I knew I needed to stay calm.

I growled, "What have you done with Cora?"

A smug smile appeared on his lips. "Not to worry, Miss Hemingway. I just need to ask you a few questions, that's all."

I wanted to leap off the couch and tear him apart with my bare hands, but I knew I couldn't. I needed to find out what was going on first, and I needed to know where Cora was.

I said, "I don't know who you are, or why you're here, but you need to tell me that Cora's okay."

Just then, there was a shuffling sound. I turned to find Cora making her way toward us, dressed in a pink frock with matching pink house shoes. She was holding a small silver tray with four steaming cups of coffee. My eyes grew as big as saucers, not only because Cora seemed to be completely oblivious to the fact that she'd allowed a crazed killer inside her home but also because tagging along right behind her, carrying her pink crutches over his shoulder, was Paco.

He said, "Hey, kiddo."

Cora said, "Of course I'm okay, dear. What did you think?"

I tried to stand up, but immediately my head started spinning. I crouched over the sofa for a second or two and then lowered myself back down. When I finally spoke, the words came out haltingly, like I was spitting watermelon seeds.

"Somebody . . . tell me . . . what's going on."

Paco handed Cora her crutches and then joined me on the left side of the couch. I was staring at him, waiting for an answer, but then I felt movement on my right. I turned to find Ethan sitting down next to me, holding a little cream pitcher in one hand and a crystal sugar bowl in the other. He put them on the table and then gave me a slightly chagrined smile, squeezing my knee with both hands.

He said, "Yeah, you might wanna stay sitting for this."

I leaned into him as he wrapped his arms around me. For a moment, I tried to block everyone else out. I pressed my cheek into his chest and shook my head. "Ethan, what the hell is happening?"

Mr. Scotland stirred a spoonful of sugar into his coffee cup. He said, "She's a wee bit *doilt*, I think."

"And what is *he* doing here?" I sat up and searched Ethan's face for answers. "Or for that matter, what are *you* doing here?"

Paco said, "Dixie, you told Michael you'd meet him at the firehouse. He called me and Ethan when you didn't show up. We were all worried where you'd gone, so Ethan just made an educated guess." He glanced at Cora. "Turns out he was right."

Cora said, "I'm sorry, Dixie, but you know very well once you get an idea in your head it's damn near impossible to shake it."

I said, "*What* idea in my head?"

Paco said, "It was just too dangerous to let you go running off into the night alone. Ethan had a feeling you might come here, so we gave Cora a call and asked her to try to keep you here."

"By any means necessary," Cora said with just a tinge of guilt in her voice. "Those were his exact words."

"By any means . . ." I glanced at my empty teacup, which was still sitting on the coffee table from the night before. "No . . ."

"I slipped you a Mickey." Cora turned to Mr. Scotland. "I believe that's what you spy types call it?"

Mr. Scotland said, "Sure."

I gasped, "You *drugged* me with your pain pills?"

"Well, Dixie, somebody needed to knock some sense into you."

"Cora! You didn't knock some sense into me—you knocked me out!"

She waved her hand in the air. "I know. And you can be angry if you want, but as soon as Paco told me what was going on, I knew I didn't have a choice. You'd have done the same thing yourself, and you know it."

I turned to Ethan. "Did you know she drugged me?"

A slight smile played across his lips. "No, not until I got here, but I have to say, I'm kind of . . ."

I waited. "Kind of . . . ?"

"I'm kind of glad she did."

Mr. Scotland said, "But it's ower noo. We cot the bass."

My eyes narrowed as I turned to Paco. "Who is this man, and what did he just say?"

Paco smiled. "This is Rupert Wolff. He's a U.S. marshal. I believe he's saying you've got nothing to worry about now. We caught the 'gentleman' who was after you. He was downstairs in your car."

My eyes widened. "He was *what*?"

Ethan said, "It's okay. He put up a fight, but they got him. He followed you here last night, and they found him hiding in your car. He was crouched down in the backseat, holding a . . ."

His voice faltered.

I turned to Paco. "What was he holding?"

Paco said, "A butcher knife in one hand, and a note in the other . . ."

"A note . . ."

He nodded. "It said, 'Goodbye, Dixie.'"

I took a deep breath and tried to stay as calm as possible, but immediately I felt the blood drain from my cheeks. Ethan pulled me in a little closer.

Cora said, "Oh, sweetheart. Let me see if I can find something to make you feel better."

"Forget it," I said. "I'm not touching a thing you put in front of me ever again."

She rolled her eyes as she headed for the kitchen. "Oh, please. Don't be such a drama queen."

I turned to Paco, "So, who is he? Why was he after me?"

Mr. Scotland set his cup down and leveled me with his piercing blue eyes. "He's a hired killer. An assassin. And if you ask me, a might strong one for such an old codger."

Paco said, "Dixie, he wasn't really after you. Agent Wolff was sent here because . . ." He glanced up at Cora as she disappeared around the corner of the kitchen and then lowered his voice. "Elba Kramer's husband was under federal protection. His name is Albert Greco."

My mouth dropped open. "You mean, as in, *witness* protection?"

Mr. Scotland nodded. "Ten years ago, Albert Greco was arrested in Baltimore for arms trafficking. He copped a deal for immunity and ratted out all his friends. As a result, a lot of very nasty people went to jail, people that wanted him dead. He's been in hiding ever since, but a few weeks ago, we intercepted phone calls that suggested there was a plan under way to assassinate him. With help from Paco's team at Special Investigations, we set up shop in the house across the street. We thought we still had time to relocate him, but things moved much faster than we expected."

At some point while he was talking, I realized Mr. Scotland's accent had completely faded away. I said, "But I don't understand. What does any of this have to do with me? What about Sara Potts? And Edith Reed?"

Mr. Scotland's eyes softened. "We have reason to believe that the deaths of those two women were, unfortunately, collateral in nature. The killer left those notes on their bodies to throw us off the trail. They wanted the whole thing to look like there was someone after *you,* murdering your friends and clients one by one, torturing you . . . When they fired through that front window, their intended target was Albert Greco, but they were hoping you'd be there too, meeting with Elba Kramer and her bird."

I said, "But I wasn't. I was in the pool house."

"Yes, and in all likelihood, had Deputy Morgan not been there to complicate things, the gunman would have gone through the house looking for you. Afterward, he planned to place that last note on your body."

I muttered, "*Goodbye, Dixie.*"

"That's right. But of course as soon as Deputy Morgan opened fire, he couldn't finish the job. He had to run. That's why he followed you here last night. And that's why he was hiding in your car with a knife."

I shuddered. "But . . . how did they even know who I was?"

"We're not sure, but we think perhaps Elba Kramer's phone was tapped."

I shook my head in disbelief. "And the guy in my car, where is he now?"

Paco said, "At the station. Detective Carthage is interrogating him as we speak. But the main thing is, no one's after you. You're safe."

"So, basically, you guys saved my life."

Paco tipped his chin at Cora, who was making her way back into the living room. "I believe you have Cora to thank for that."

Cora was carrying a wooden cutting board in the middle of which was a freshly baked loaf of chocolate bread. She put it down on the coffee table in front of us, and immediately the room filled with the sweet aroma of everything that's good in the world.

Her eyes sparkling, she said, "Who likes chocolate?"

26

When I was little, lots of my girlfriends fantasized about their wedding day. They'd drape long white sheets over their heads and two-step around their bedrooms, hugging a wilted bouquet of wildflowers to their budding chests and beaming at their imaginary husbands. I never really understood it. Sure, I saw myself married with a husband and kids, but I never put a whole lot of stock in the actual marriage ceremony, which is why, after I pulled into the parking lot of the Kitty Haven, I was somewhat surprised at myself. I wasn't thinking about Albert Greco or Elba Kramer. I wasn't thinking about Sara Potts or Edith Reed. And I wasn't thinking about the hired assassin that had been waiting in my car with a butcher knife . . . I was thinking about Guidry's wedding.

I'd left Cora's apartment with the intention of going home for a shower and a change of clothes, but on the way there I'd gotten word the investigation crew was done with Caroline's house, which meant I could finally take Franklin and Gigi home. I knew it would make me feel better to put at least one thing back to normal, but just as I was about to get out of the car, I glanced at the time. Guidry's wedding was happening right that very minute.

I leaned back in the seat and closed my eyes, thinking I'd just sit there and rest for a bit, but almost immediately I saw him.

Guidry.

Waiting at the altar.

Surrounded by friends and family . . . beaming.

I could see him as clearly as if I was standing there myself. He was dressed in a sharp black tuxedo and bow tie, gazing at the doorway from which his soon-to-be wife would emerge, his steady eyes dark gray, edging toward blue. In my mind, I turned and gazed at the doorway too, practically holding my breath, waiting to see who was about to come through it—Monacle or Monochrome or whatever her name is.

In the front room of the Kitty Haven, Jaz was sitting on her knees in the middle of the carpet, waving two bamboo sticks in the air like a deranged traffic controller. Each stick had a string with a tuft of peacock feathers tied to the end, and there were about a dozen cats leaping after them like kernels of corn in a hot skillet. I've never heard anyone say it out loud, but a group of cats is called a clowder, which sounds more like something you'd eat with a spoon and some saltine crackers. In this case, though, the cats were making such a spectacle of themselves that it actually seemed appropriate. Meanwhile, Gigi was nestled in Jaz's lap, watching the complicated cat choreography with rapt attention, as perfectly still as only a bunny can be.

I found Franklin in his kitty suite down the hall, watching a movie about mice running through a maze, and despite the fact that he didn't seem particularly happy to see me, he purred in my arms all the way out to the Bronco. I think he was looking forward to getting back home where he belonged, and while Gigi didn't say as much, I knew he felt the same way.

Driving to Caroline's, I tried not to think about anything other than getting back to my regular routine. Thanks to Cora and her "secret ingredient," I'd slept like a drunken baby, and that—combined with a cup of coffee and a slice or five of Cora's mouth-watering chocolate bread—was starting to make me feel a little more energized.

Plus, I could acknowledge it now: I wasn't afraid. For the first time in days, I wasn't looking over my shoulder to see who was following me. I wasn't calculating my every move, expecting a homicidal maniac to jump out from every corner. I felt like myself again.

Well . . . almost.

Something was still nagging at me, like a thorn lodged in the back of my brain, and, try as I might, I couldn't shake it loose. For one, I kept thinking about Elba Kramer. I couldn't imagine what she must have been going through. To have lost her husband, and in such a violent, horrible way. And to have discovered his body . . .

That poor woman, I thought to myself.

Elba seemed to enjoy her reputation for being wild and independent, but there was an unmistakable fragility about her, something unsteady at her core. I had a feeling she might be utterly lost without her husband to help keep her grounded.

Caroline's house was completely back to normal, as if nothing had ever happened, but Elba's house was a different story. There was an unmarked sedan parked in the front, with two deputy cruisers and a mobile forensics van, and the entire property was surrounded with police tape. On the front gate, gleaming like yellow butterflies in the sunlight, were half a dozen evidence markers flapping in the breeze.

I pulled into Caroline's driveway and tried not to look at the house across the street where Mr. Scotland had set up camp. I think I was hoping I might be able to get inside without talking to anybody. I balanced Franklin and Gigi in their matching cat carriers, one in each hand, and kept my head down all the way to the house.

As soon as I unlocked the door, I remembered Charlie racing down the hallway with his leash trailing behind him. I'd forgotten to call a painter about having that door repaired, but I doubted Caroline would give a hoot about a few scratches when she found out everything else that had happened while she'd been away.

Franklin slinked out of his cage and wasted no time letting me know what he thought about being locked up in a box. Most cats have a vocabulary of at least a hundred different meows, each with its own particular intonation and meaning, but they rarely meow at each other. Instead, that finely tuned language is reserved almost exclusively for humans. He meowed at me all the way down the hall, making a beeline for Caroline's bedroom without so much as a "Thanks for the lift!" or "Smell ya later!" I didn't mind, though. I knew he'd feel better once he got back into his regular routine.

Gigi, on the other hand, was downright giddy. As soon as I plopped him down in his mansion-cage, he went hopping through every room, exploring every corner and dancing a binky on each level, occasionally doubling back to make sure I was watching. Once he was sure everything was in order, he skipped through his raceway and went out to inspect the lanai.

It was a glorious day. The sun was just reaching its peak, and the leaves of the lime trees surrounding the pool were trembling gently in the breeze off the ocean. I sat down next to the pool, and immediately Gigi climbed into my lap. By the hopeful look in his eye, I knew exactly what he was after.

I said, "Gigi, I've had a rough week. Do you really think I had time to think about your needs?"

He wiggled his whiskers and took one tiny hop forward.

I reached into my pocket. "Well, you're right."

I handed him a carrot stick, which he took with both paws and then settled into the crook of my elbow, nibbling away like a tiny cottontailed wood chipper.

"You're welcome."

Just then, the bushes along the side of the house separated, and for a split second my heart sped up by a factor of about a thousand. It was Detective Carthage. He stepped up to the screen door and flipped his bangs away from his eyes. "I imagine Ms. Greaver's pets are happy to be home, huh?"

I mustered a smile as I put Gigi down and stood up. "Yeah, especially this little guy. He's got much better digs here."

Gigi hopped a couple of feet toward Detective Carthage but then changed his mind and headed for his raceway. There were a couple of awkward moments of silence as we watched him scamper off, but then Detective Carthage cleared his throat.

He said, "Miss Hemingway, I'm sure I'm the last person you want to talk to right now, but . . ."

I held up one hand to stop him. "I know. I owe you an apology for running off the way I did. I'm sorry. I really am. I just felt like I'd run out of options."

He tipped his head to one side. "Yeah, about that. Did you know it's considered a crime to flee the scene of a homicide?"

I nodded, although *flee* seemed like an awfully strong word.

"And did you know it's considered a crime to elude an officer of the law?"

I crossed my arms over my chest. "Yeah. But did you know it's considered stupid to wait around and see if a serial killer might murder you?"

He grinned and tossed his hair again. "Yeah. I have to admit you've got a point there. Umm . . . how are you?"

"I'm fine, I think." I slid my hands down in my pockets. "I'm glad it's all over. I'm not exactly sure I've had time to process the whole thing. How is Ms. Kramer?"

He glanced over his shoulder. "Not good, actually. She's holed up in the pool house. We're trying to convince her to leave, to check in to a hotel or something, but she just wants to be left alone. I think she's in shock, which is understandable, but also . . . well, I don't think she has that many friends."

"Has she eaten anything?"

"I don't know. Her assistant . . ." He paused for a moment.

"Rajinder?"

"Yes. He stopped by earlier. He took some food over, but I doubt she's touched it."

My stomach tightened. I couldn't help but imagine the horror of what Elba Kramer must have seen when she ran into that front room. And then out of nowhere I sensed that sickly sweet smell again—very faint, like a distant memory—but enough to make me think I was doomed for the rest of my life to smell perfume whenever the idea of murder came up.

I said, "I wish there was something I could do to help."

He looked down, and I noticed he was holding a pair of bright blue rubber gloves. "Well, as a matter of fact, I was wondering if you might help me convince Ms. Kramer she should leave the house during the investigation. I think she might listen to you."

"Why would you think that?"

"She told me the two of you have a long history together . . . ?"

I nodded. "Oh, that."

"But also, it would help with the investigation if you took a walk through the house with me."

I said, "What investigation? I mean, they caught the killer . . . right?"

He said, "Yes, but not the people who hired him. And we think they may have had help from the inside."

I thought of Rajinder and how sweet he'd been with Charlie. Was it possible Carthage thought he was involved somehow? And then there was the gardener. I'd seen her trimming the hedge when I walked up to the front door, but I hadn't gotten a good look at her face. I wondered if Carthage had already questioned her.

I took a deep breath and sighed.

I doubted Elba would listen to me, and I definitely didn't want to see the room where Albert Greco had been killed, and I honestly didn't think anything I'd seen could help them find whoever it was that had betrayed Elba and her husband.

But, then again, I've spent a lot of time with cats, watching their movements, observing their hunting techniques, studying the way they home in on their target with every cell—from the tips of their tails to the point of every quivering whisker . . .

And if there's one thing I know how to do, it's sniff out a rat.

27

I was standing on the back patio next to Detective Carthage, just beyond one of the big vine-covered columns. The sun was bouncing off the surface of the pool, sending rippling ribbons of light everywhere—completely at odds with the somber mood that lay like a fog over the entire Kramer residence.

It was entirely silent.

Usually, investigators and crime technicians mill about chatting freely, as if they find themselves at the scene of a crime every day, which of course they just about do. But the half dozen or so men and women moving around the property were dead quiet, and I wondered if it wasn't out of respect for Ms. Kramer, who was still sitting by herself in the pool house with her canary.

I could see my reflection in the long glass wall of the living room, and I'm ashamed to admit that I noted how ridiculous I looked—still dressed in the same clothes I'd had on the day before, my hair a squirrel's nest, not to mention the blue rubber gloves and the face mask that

Detective Carthage had asked me to put on—neither of which made sense, by the way. He wasn't wearing a mask, and I knew not to touch anything, plus I was pretty sure my fingerprints and DNA were all over the place, so it wasn't like I could contaminate any evidence. Detective Carthage was still new on the job, though, so I figured he was probably just following the rules to the letter.

He said, "Ms. Kramer has done her best to fill me in on what she remembers, but it would be helpful if you could tell me what you saw. I know it's difficult, but every detail, no matter how trivial it may seem, can be helpful. These situations are always hard, but I promise you're safe. I'll be with you every step of the way."

I tried not to cringe. He sounded like he was reading right out of a college textbook on the proper handling of a crime-scene witness, but I didn't want to embarrass him. I just nodded politely as he rambled on.

Inside, there were a couple of men in the hallway at the front of the house, covered from head to toe in white hazmat suits. One of them had just come out of the study and was headed straight for us, walking along a line of white drop cloths laid on the floor. As soon as I saw what he was carrying, I should have looked away, but I couldn't stop myself.

It was a plastic bag, about the size you'd use for a kitchen trash bin, except the plastic was see-through and much thicker. Inside was a matted mess of cardboard, full of ragged holes and soaked in dark, red blood. It seemed to glimmer in the sun, as if it had been sprinkled with sequins. Just then, I felt the curling tendrils of that sweet flowery scent start to wend their way into my brain. I put my hand out on the column to steady myself and mumbled, "Oh, please. Not again . . ."

Carthage said, "You alright?"

I shook my head, trying to shake the scent away as I pulled the mask off my face. "I don't know what's wrong with me but . . . it's this smell. I keep—"

"Yeah, I know," he interrupted. "I should have warned you." He pulled a face mask out of his back pocket. "I don't even smell it anymore. Believe me, it's much better now than it was yesterday."

"Wait. What are you talking about?"

"The smell. That's why I gave you that mask. Our crime cleanup crew is pretty good, but I don't think they have a whole lot of experience when it comes to getting rid of perfume."

I blinked. "Perfume. What perfume?"

His eyes widened. "Follow me."

He led the way inside, staying in the middle of the white tarps, and I followed about five feet behind him. The closer we got to the front hall, the stronger the smell got, and by the time we stopped at the door to the study, I'd already guessed what had happened. It was those boxes I'd seen, stacked on top of the desk, plastered all over with red and white FRAGILE stickers.

Detective Carthage said, "According to Rajinder, there'd been a delivery that afternoon, not long before you arrived to meet Ms. Kramer. About five cases, from Paris. Normally, they would've been sent to the shop downtown, but there was a mix-up. Mr. Greco had just started unpacking them when . . ."

I stepped into the doorway and gasped.

For the most part, the room looked the same as I remembered it—the wall of leather-bound books, the Persian rug, the antique desk with the green armchair and the big boxy television behind it—except, now, almost every inch of it was riddled with bullet holes. There were two industrial-size flood lamps on tripods just inside the doorway, filling the room with white light and illuminating spatters of blood on almost every surface.

Detective Carthage said, "From the position of his body, we believe he attempted to crawl over his desk for the door as soon as the gunfire started, but he didn't stand a chance."

I nodded mutely. I've never been that squeamish around blood, but it took all my concentration just to keep my balance. On the desk, surrounded by several disintegrated boxes, was a leather blotter with a large dark stain at its center . . .

And then there was the glass.

It was everywhere—tiny shards that sparkled like glitter in the harsh light. If I hadn't known better, I'd have thought they were diamonds and not the shattered remains of French perfume bottles.

As Detective Carthage pulled his cell phone out of his back pocket, I let out a heavy shudder and massaged the space between my eyebrows with the tips of my fingers. That sweet smell was almost overwhelming—a thick, heady melange of magnolia, jasmine, and honeysuckle. I could almost taste it on my tongue.

Carthage looked concerned. "You okay?"

"Nothing. I just kept smelling it. This whole time,

I thought it was my imagination. It reminded me of the magnolia tree in my driveway, where they found Mrs. Reed's body . . . I thought I was losing my mind."

His lips tightened into a vague smirk, as if the status of my mental stability was still open for discussion, and then he tapped at his cell phone. A cartoon-like image of a microphone appeared on the screen as he held it out in the space between us.

"This is Detective Matthew Carthage with the Sarasota Sheriff's Department. The time is twelve forty-five P.M. I'm at the home of Elba Kramer and Albert Greco, in the room where Albert Greco was murdered." He turned to me. "Can you state your name, please?"

I frowned. "Huh?"

"I'm recording our interview. I just need you to state your name for the record."

I cleared my throat, suddenly feeling like a suspect. "Dixie Hemingway."

"Middle name?"

I paused.

No one knows my middle name, and I mean *no one.* I keep it safely guarded. In fact, normally Carthage would've needed to pull out every interrogation trick he'd learned in detective school to get it out of me—including any "enhanced techniques" he'd picked up along the way—but I think at that point I was a little off my game.

I said, "Sue."

He leaned forward. "Sorry?"

"Sue!" I tried my best to make it sound like a powerful

name—something commanding and respectable—instead of like the name of a prim and prissy Southern belle. "Dixie *Sue* Hemingway."

"Okay. Can you please describe what you saw when you arrived here yesterday?"

I told him how Ms. Kramer had met me at the door, how I'd gotten a glimpse of her husband in the study, and how she'd said he wasn't feeling too "social," as she'd put it. And I told him how Ms. Kramer had lowered the living room windows into the floor, and how she'd asked Rajinder to go pick up a prescription for her.

"Did she say what the prescription was for?"

"No."

"And did you see Rajinder leave the house?"

"No. I just remember Elba—I mean, Ms. Kramer— telling him he needed to hurry because the pharmacy closed at six. I didn't see him again."

"And did he seem nervous at all? Or distracted?"

"No. Not that I could tell. But I'd only met him the one time before, so I can't say for sure. You don't think he had something to do with this, do you?"

He shrugged slightly. "Elba Kramer had a lot of people in and out of the property—repairmen, hair stylists, assistants, etcetera. Until we have all the facts, I'm not closing any doors. Do you recall seeing anyone else in the house while you were here?"

I said, "Yes. When I first arrived, there was a woman in the front yard. The gardener. She was pruning those tall shrubs in the front."

Carthage frowned, "Did you talk to her?"

"No. But Ms. Kramer said she was like a member of the family."

"When was this?"

"When we were sitting in the living room. Rajinder had brought in some iced tea, and she said it was made with mint from the garden."

He nodded. "The gardener's name is Sally Ridge. She's worked for Mr. Greco about ten years. She started out as a maid, but she hurt her back in a car accident, so now she helps with the garden, runs errands, shopping, etcetera."

While he was talking, my eyes had fallen on a tiny yellow feather that lay at the edge of the Persian carpet closest to the door. About three feet farther in were two more feathers, one right next to the other, and then beyond that were a few more. I followed the line they made all the way across the carpet to the far wall of the study, where there was a large window—or, rather, what *remained* of a large window. Its splintered panes were hanging in pieces, some held in place only by the shards of glass that still clung to them, swinging gently in the breeze from outside. Along the top of the window was a brass bar, draped with folds of maroon velvet curtains so thick they would normally have blocked out every ounce of daylight, but midway down there was nothing left of them but tattered, bullet-torn shreds.

"Mrs. Hemingway?"

"Huh?"

"I asked what happened after you had tea . . . ?"

"Sorry. I zoned out there for a minute . . . This is kind

of overwhelming. Ms. Kramer was showing me around the pool house when it happened, but . . ."

He nodded. "I know. She could easily have brought you in this room first. Those curtains were closed when the gunman opened fire, so he was essentially shooting blind, but he made up for that with the sheer number of bullets he unloaded. From the pattern of the damage, we can tell he made at least three passes: one at chest level, one about waist height, and another along the floor. In other words, he made sure no one in this room got out alive. Well, that is, except . . ."

He directed my attention to the top left corner of the window, where there was a brass chain about three feet long hanging from the ceiling. A gold hoop, roughly three inches in diameter, dangled at its end.

"That birdcage would've been right above eye level."

I said, "Which means . . ."

"Which means it just missed being blown to smithereens."

I stared at the empty space where the cage would have been. Carthage was right. About a foot or so below the brass hoop, the velvet curtains hung in threads, but above they were completely intact.

I couldn't think of anything else to say, except, "Wow."

"Yeah. That's one lucky canary."

"Yeah . . ."

I turned away from the window to face him. Over his shoulder I could see the doorway into the room across the hall. I heard his voice echo in my head. *Until we have all the facts, I'm not closing any doors.*

He held his phone out again, and I noticed there was

a little red timer on the screen, ticking away just under the cartoon microphone. "So, Mrs. Hemingway, how long would you say you were sitting in the living room before Ms. Kramer took you over to the pool house?"

I said, "Yeah," and stepped around him into the hall.

The room directly opposite the office was a guest bedroom. There was a queen-size bed with an orange-and-yellow striped comforter spread across it, and on the far wall was a white-lacquered dresser with a fringed lamp on top. I could tell the room didn't get used much. It seemed a little empty compared with the rest of the house. Plus, there were a few boxes sitting on the bed and a couple more stacked against the wall on the side of the dresser. There was another box standing open at the foot of the bed with a box cutter lying next to it, and inside were stacks of clear plastic boxes with various pieces of jewelry inside—brooches, bracelets, earrings— nothing that looked particularly expensive, but I could tell it was probably all handmade.

There was also a little wire birdcage on the dresser, with a single sheet of newspaper laid underneath. Attached to the side of the cage on the inside was a small acrylic-coated mirror, along with a plastic yellow perch and matching feed cups. The whole thing looked cheap and flimsy, like something you might pick up at a discount market or a dollar store. I figured it was probably the cage Ms. Kramer's bird had come in when she bought it.

I turned to find Detective Carthage standing in the open doorway behind me. He had a slightly annoyed look on his face.

"Mrs. Hemingway, why do I think you're not listening to me?"

I could feel my jaw tightening. I said, "Yesterday, when Ms. Kramer was showing me around the house, I didn't see this room."

"Yes . . . ?"

I looked down. To the left of the doorway, lying in a wadded heap on the floor, was a thin cotton sheet. It was dark navy blue and small, like something for a child's bed or a crib.

I said, "I didn't see this room because this door was closed."

He frowned slightly. "So . . . what are you saying?"

I don't know why I hadn't thought of it before, but it was like something had clicked in my head. Or, more precisely, like my mind had been trapped in a deep, dark cave, miles underground, and someone had switched on a lightbulb . . . right in front of my face.

I felt my eyebrows creep up my forehead as I lowered my voice to a whisper.

"Is Rajinder still with Ms. Kramer?"

He shook his head. "He left a while ago. Why?"

I said, "I think we better go check on her."

28

The first thing I saw when I opened the door to the pool house was Jane, Ms. Kramer's canary, perched inside her gold birdcage all alone on the long glass coffee table in the living area. As I closed the door behind me, she pivoted her head from side to side and eyed me suspiciously.

There was a palpable stillness in the room. I took a couple of steps forward and tried to swallow, but my throat was so tight I could barely manage it. I peered down the hallway toward the spa area, but there was nothing I could see that would indicate anyone was there.

I stepped back slowly to the door and then heard a muffled sigh.

Elba Kramer was slumped in the near corner of the white leather sofa, still dressed in the linen slacks and gauzy blouse she'd worn when I first met her, although now there was a rust-colored smear on her right cuff. I realized with a shiver it was probably dried blood. On the floor between the sofa and the coffee table was a wineglass next to an almost empty bottle of red wine.

As I stepped closer, she opened her eyes.

"Hello, Dixie."

I let out a sigh of relief and sat down in one of the chairs opposite her. "Hi, Ms. Kramer. How are you doing?"

She nodded. "Everyone keeps asking me that."

"Sorry. Dumb question, I know. I came over to talk to you because . . . well, I was speaking with Detective Carthage, and there was something he wanted me to ask you."

She let her head fall back against the sofa, and I noticed there were watery trails of mascara running down her cheeks. "They're trying to get rid of me, I know. I just needed a little more time here. This was our home for so long, Albert and me. It's hard to imagine walking away without him. There were so many things we still wanted to do. So many plans . . ." Tears sprung to her eyes. "I still can't believe it."

I leaned forward. "Elba, I wish there was something I could tell you that would help."

She shook her head and smiled. "You're so sweet. But don't worry about me. I'm pretty good at dealing with this kind of stuff . . . I've been through hard times before. I'll survive. I just wanted to sit here a little while longer, in the home we built together. I have a feeling once I leave I'll never come back. Although I get it. I really do. I'm just in the way here. And the sooner I'm gone, the sooner the detectives can figure out what happened . . . why anyone would want to hurt us."

I hesitated, ". . . yeah."

She studied me for a moment, and then something softened in her face. "How much do you know?"

I figured there was no point trying to keep anything from her. I said, "I know you and your husband were in the witness protection program and that some very bad people were looking for you . . ."

"So, you're not really a cat sitter are you?" She nodded slowly. "I suspected as much."

"Huh?"

"Believe me, I'm not surprised." She dabbed at her eyes with the hem of her blouse. "You seem a little too smart for that. You're a U.S. marshal then?"

"No, no. Ms. Kramer, I really am a cat sitter."

She frowned. "Then . . . how do you know about Albert and me?"

I said, "Last night, after I left here, a man followed me to a friend's house. The cops found him hiding in my car with a butcher knife. He planned on killing me, just like he killed those other two women . . . just like he killed your husband."

Her eyelids fluttered as she shook her head. "Wait. I don't understand."

"The woman that was found next door at Caroline's house, Sara Potts, and the woman that was found in my driveway, Edith Reed, they were murdered to make it look like your husband's death was part of a plan to kill me."

Her lips parted slightly as her hands went to the center of her chest. "No . . . No, that's not possible."

"I'm afraid it is. They were hoping it would throw the detectives off their track."

"But . . ." She brought her hands together and pressed them to her lips, suddenly looking like a young girl praying at the side of her bed. "I'm sorry . . . I'm just speechless . . ."

I said, "That's understandable. The thing is . . . Elba, why did you hire me?"

"To take care of Jane, of course."

"Yes, that's what you said, but why? I mean, were you planning on going somewhere?"

She sat forward. "Wait a minute. Are you suggesting I had something to do with all this?"

I could feel my heart racing. "I am. Ms. Kramer, you knew that gunman was coming, didn't you?"

"No . . . that's completely ridiculous."

"And you wanted me here when it happened. That way, when they found my dead body in that front room, they'd think I was the target, and they'd think your husband was just collateral damage . . . especially when they found that note."

"*Note?* What note?"

"The note the gunman planned to leave on my body after I was dead. They found it in his pocket when they caught him hiding in my car. It was written on the same paper as the notes they found on those two other women, pinned to their bodies with a pearl-tipped hat pin, which I would guess probably came from your shop. It said, 'Goodbye, Dixie,' but you probably already knew that."

"Wait a minute . . ." She stopped, trying to find the right words, her mouth open, her eyes searching my face. I had to hand it to her. She was pretty convincing. If her career as a murderous, gold-digging model hadn't panned out, she could very well have been a successful actress. "Dixie, I swear to you, I have no idea what this is about."

I shook my head. "I think you do. And I think you're the one who told those mobsters where they could find your husband."

"No. That's insane. Why would I do something so stupid?"

"I imagine you probably cut some kind of deal with them to spare your life . . . in exchange for the location of your husband."

She stiffened. "Who in the world gave you that idea? One of those detectives?"

I looked down at Jane, who had hopped up on her perch and was bobbing her head back and forth as if she somehow sensed the tension in the room.

"No," I said. "Jane did."

Ms. Kramer stood up and pointed at the door. "You're crazy. I want you out of this house. *Now.*"

I said, "No. You intentionally put my life in danger. I'm not leaving until you tell me the truth."

She said, "I *am* telling you the truth! I don't know anything about those two other women. I don't know about any notes. I don't know about any man hiding in your car. And I certainly don't know about any crazy plot involving you. I just lost my husband! Does that mean nothing?" She picked up the birdcage and hugged it to her chest as Jane fluttered to keep her balance inside. "Get out of my house now, or I'll have those cops throw you out!"

My legs were trembling. I took another deep breath and tried to maintain my composure. I said, "Ms.

Kramer, this whole time I thought it was a miracle Jane made it out of that room alive—there were so many bullets—but then I saw where her cage was, and it all made sense . . ."

She said, "It *was* a miracle. I don't know what I would have done if . . ."

"No," I interrupted. "I mean the *other* cage. The one in the guest bedroom . . . the one Jane was in when that gunman opened fire."

She shook her head. "Jane wasn't in that cage. She was in this one. You saw me carry her out of my husband's study yourself."

"I did. And to be honest, with all the confusion at the time, I barely noticed the door to the guest room. I specifically remember it was closed when you showed me into the house. But after the gunfire, when you came out of the study carrying Jane, that guest room door was wide open. Elba . . . you forgot to close it."

She stared at me for what seemed like an eternity, and then something broke in her expression, something almost undetectable—just the slightest shift in the muscles of her face. All the fire that had shone in her eyes was gone now, and she seemed utterly deflated.

She lowered herself back down on the couch and balanced the cage in her lap, staring at Jane as she spoke. "Miss Hemingway, I'm very tired. Maybe Rajinder opened that door, or the gardener, or, for that matter, maybe Albert opened it himself. We may never know. But, by all means, if you think I ratted out my own husband, if you think I'm responsible for his murder—all because you saw a goddamn open door—then, please, run and tell your detective friends right now. But leave me in peace. I'm done talking."

I wanted to get out of there as much as she wanted me out, but I couldn't go. Not yet. This woman had pulled me into a trap, like a spider lures its victim into a web, and I needed to hear her say it.

I said, "It wasn't the door that got me thinking. It was something else. After we heard those gunshots, you ran away from me as fast as you could. You ran right into the house, and you went straight to the guest bedroom. You took Jane out of that extra cage, and then you went across the hall into your husband's office, where you put her in the cage she's in now, the one that was hanging in front of that window. Then you took the cage down and rushed back out, completely ignoring your husband's dying body only a few feet away. I'd guess you were in that room no more than ten seconds."

While I spoke, Elba had dropped her chin. I could see tears rolling down her cheeks, forming wet circles where they fell on the front of her blouse. Staring at Jane, she shrugged slightly. "Oh, really? And why is that?"

I said, "Ms. Kramer, all birds are sensitive creatures, but a bird like Jane is especially vulnerable. I'm sure you know there are all kinds of things that could make her respiratory system shut down. Things like gas from a barbecue grill, or car exhaust, or even seemingly harmless things, like fumes from household cleaners, or, in large enough amounts . . ."

She nodded slowly. "Perfume."

"Yes. Perfume. It would have been a miracle if Jane had survived that gunfire, but to have lived more than ten seconds with all that perfume in the air . . . Elba, it's impossible."

She looked up, her lips parted slightly. "Well, I said you were smart, didn't I? But you're wrong about one thing: I didn't ignore my husband's body. It was the most horrible thing that's ever happened to me . . ."

There was a tiny wisp of yellow down clinging to the arm of the sofa next to her. She picked it up between her thumb and forefinger and studied it closely. "It had to be done, though. It was only a matter of time. Those men were after him . . . but they would have killed us both. The only way I could save myself was to help them find him."

I could barely believe she'd changed her tune so quickly, without even a moment's hesitation. For a split second, I thought perhaps she was mocking me.

I said, "So . . . it's true?"

She looked down at her hands. "Albert's always in his study, so I knew that was where he'd be that afternoon, and they promised it would be fast . . . and painless. I just didn't plan on that shipment. I sent Rajinder to the pharmacy to get him out of the house. I didn't want poor Raji to get hurt too."

I said, "Lucky him. I'm guessing the gunman showed up a little early, or otherwise you'd have already sent me into that office with your husband."

She raised her eyes and stared at me imploringly. "Dixie, I swear I don't know a thing about any kind of plot involving you or those two other women. Think about it. If I'd meant for you to be killed, why would I have brought you over here to the pool house?"

I shook my head. "I have no idea. But then, why did you bring me here at all, when you knew those gunmen were on their way?"

She looked at Jane and sighed. "I needed a witness."

"A *witness*?"

"I'm sorry, honey. I really am, but I didn't have a choice. I knew they'd suspect me first. Who else? Other than a handful of U.S. marshals, I'm the only person alive who could've told Albert's enemies where he was, so I had to do everything I could to look innocent. For one, I knew I had to be here when it happened. It would've looked suspicious if I'd left the house right before. And I knew I had to act as if it was just another regular day."

I put my hands on my hips. "So you brought me over here so I could tell everyone how normal you seemed right before the murder . . ."

She nodded.

". . . and how shocked you were after."

"That was the idea, yes. Pretending to have Jane in the room with Albert was just an extra precaution on my part. I figured no one would think I'd leave her in there if I'd known what was about to happen. Everyone knows how much I love her."

I shook my head. I couldn't quite put my finger on it, but there was something about her story that just didn't add up. I said, "No. You're lying. You planned on sending me into that room to be killed with your husband, and you knew they were going to put that note on my body after. I can see it in your eyes. I think you chick-ened out at the last minute and didn't want the blood of one more innocent victim on your hands, or maybe that gunman arrived earlier than planned. Either way, it doesn't matter—in the eyes of the law, you've conspired to commit murder. I'm sorry, Elba, but you're going to jail."

She took a deep breath and then smiled sadly. "No. I'm not going anywhere. Nobody saw me come out of that room but you, Dixie. I was already standing in the hallway when that deputy burst through the front door. I'll just tell everyone you got it wrong, that Jane's cage wasn't hanging in Albert's office at all. It was in the guest room the whole time."

I shook my head. "No. There was blood on that cage. I saw it when you came out, and I'm sure the deputy saw it too. How will you explain that?"

She tilted her head to one side. "Good point. Oh, I just remembered! I ran into Albert's office first and grabbed his arm to see if he was alive, and then I ran into the guest room. When I grabbed Jane's cage, I realized there was blood on my hands . . ." Her eyes traveled down my body and then back up again, as if she was judging a piece of cheap furniture. "See how that works? Trust me, honey. I'll win. There's no one on earth who would take a cat sitter's word over mine."

Her words stung, even though, at that point, I had a pretty good reason to think she was wrong. My voice low, I said, "How can you possibly live with yourself after this?"

She flicked her hand dismissively and then slid Jane's cage closer. "Oh my God, you're so judgmental. Walk a mile in my shoes and then let's talk. And, anyway, I learned a long time ago, the best way to enjoy this world is to lower your standards." She looked at me and raised an eyebrow. "You should try it. You'd be a lot more fun if you did."

I took a deep breath. There are a lot of things I could have said at that point, like, "No one will believe you," or "You'll never get away with this," but in a strange way, I felt sorry for the woman, despite the fact that she'd had a hand in two murders, three if you counted her husband, *four* if you factored in how close I'd come to . . .

But I didn't want to think about that.

Instead, I turned away without saying another word and went to the door. Before I left, I took one last look at the Scarlet Woman of Siesta Key. She was slumped in the couch again, except now Jane's cage was in her lap, and she was pulling her hair down in strings over her face. I figured she probably wanted to look as pitiful as possible when Detective Carthage came in to talk to her.

He was waiting outside by the pool with his hands thrust down in his jean pockets and his long blond bangs pushed to one side. There were creases in the space between his eyes that I hadn't noticed before, and I wondered if he had any idea how much this job would age him.

He said, "What happened?"

I shrugged slightly. "She told me no one would take my word over hers, so . . ."

I reached into the side pocket of my cargo shorts and carefully pulled out his phone, which still had the cartoon image of a microphone on its screen, along with the little red timer underneath . . . counting off the minutes it had been recording.

29

By the time I poured myself into the driver's seat of the Bronco and headed home, it was almost five o'clock in the afternoon. I stared at the road in a kind of stupor, practically letting the car drive herself. Hung low in the pale blue sky to the east was a daytime moon—or what my grandmother always called a child's moon, since kids should be fast asleep when the moon is usually out. To the west, the sun had stained the clouds crimson, while ribbons of tangerine and yellow ochre burned like embers along the ocean's horizon.

I switched on the radio and sped through all the classic rock and Christian talk shows until I landed on one of our only remaining local stations, WULB. Officially, their broadcast range doesn't extend much farther than six or seven miles—the length of Long Boat Key, their home island north of here—but on a clear day, even the Bronco's finicky old antenna can pick it up loud and clear. Billie Holiday was on, reaching out through the airwaves with her glimmering voice, singing directly to me. Or, at least, that's how it felt . . .

The way your smile just beams,
the way you sing off key.
The way you haunt my dreams . . .
No, no! They can't take that away from me!

Just then, I looked down and saw something in the space between the center console and the passenger seat . . . It was yellow. At first, I thought it was one of Jane's feathers, which would have been perfectly reasonable since Jane was in the backseat, fluttering to balance herself inside her cheap purple birdcage. I'd strapped it in good and snug with the seat belt, but I think the ride was still a little too bumpy for her liking. Every once in a while she'd catch my eye in the rearview mirror and give me a haughty, indignant look.

At the first stoplight, I put the car in park and felt around under the passenger seat. Just as my fingers closed on something, my feeble brain sat up and shouted, *Watch out!* That gunman had been hiding in my car not much more than twenty-four hours earlier. There was no telling what he might have left behind . . .

My rational self whispered, *It might be another note!*

My inner child added, *Or a snake!*

Luckily for me, we were all wrong. As carefully as possible, I pulled it out and held it up in front of me.

It was Charlie's yellow giraffe, the one he'd brought with him that fateful evening we'd discovered Sara Potts's body. Immediately, my mind pitched back. I saw

myself sitting in the Bronco in Caroline's driveway before I went into her house, when I still thought I was
having just another perfectly normal day. I could see
Charlie too, curled up in the seat next to me with his giraffe between his paws.

While I was thinking about how much he probably
missed it (and how happy he'd be when I brought it back),
the light turned green and the car behind me honked,
scaring me so bad I let out a yelp not unlike the high-
pitched yodel of a mountain goat. I threw the Bronco in
gear and lurched forward, clutching the steering wheel
with both hands while still holding on to Charlie's giraffe.
Something about the whole situation struck a chord in
me, and I started giggling like a schoolgirl.

"Well," I said to myself. "Either you're really good at
surviving stressful situations, or you've gone completely
bonkers."

Myself replied, "Watch the road, you moron."

The car behind me moved into the oncoming lane a
couple of times, trying to get around, and then as soon
as there was an opening it revved its engine and sped by
on the left. It must have been a sight to behold—a grown
woman with wild hair, clinging to her stuffed giraffe,
giggling and talking to herself.

But I didn't care.

After what I'd been through, it felt good to laugh.
Nothing restores the mind and body more, except maybe
a nice long shower, which I planned on taking as soon
as possible. I pulled into the winding lane that leads to
our house and held my breath as I sped past the magnolia tree. I parked in the empty carport and carried Jane's

cage up the steps as smoothly as possible, and then as soon as I opened the door to my apartment, I put her down on the coffee table and started peeling off my clothes. Less than twenty seconds later I was in the shower, letting the hot water stream over my body and doing my best impersonation of Billie Holiday.

The way you hold your knife,
the way we danced till three.
The way you've changed my life . . .
No, no! They can't take that away from me!

The longer I stood there, the better I felt. All the terrible things I'd seen, all the sadness over Sara Potts and Edith Reed, all the guilt and fear and worry (not to mention the perfume) washed away, disappearing down the drain and leaving me feeling like a new woman. I must have been standing there singing at the top of my lungs for at least ten minutes when I thought I heard something on the other side of the shower curtain.

I froze.

"Dixie?"

"Ethan! Oh my gosh, you scared me to death."

He parted the curtain just wide enough to poke his head in, grinning from ear to ear and raking his eyes up and down my body. In a husky, mock soap-opera voice, he said, "Well, hello there."

Nobody likes being surprised in the shower, but all it took was one look at Ethan's beaming face to make my heart go all warm and fuzzy—I couldn't imagine being

happier to see anybody else on the planet. In fact, looking back, I must have been pretty swept up in the moment. I leaned in and gave him a wet kiss on the lips,
leaving a few drops of water dripping off his cheeks, and
then before I even knew what I was saying, the following words came spilling out of my mouth: "Hey, do you
think we should get married?"

He blinked a couple of times. "Umm . . . what did
you say?"

I raised my eyebrows. "Okay, let's not jump to any
conclusions, but I think I just proposed to you."

"Yeah. I just wanted to hear you say it again."

"I'm not sure I can."

He grinned. "That's what I thought. You better get out
of that shower. I think your brain may be waterlogged."

I stared at him. At that moment, I could easily have
shrugged it all off and turned it into a joke, but something was urging me to keep going.

I said, "Maybe, but you know, this whole thing . . . it's
got me thinking. I mean, life is just so short, you know?
Ever since Todd and Christy died, I think I've been
walking around afraid—afraid to move forward, afraid
to think about the future, just . . . *afraid*. But now . . ."

His eyes were hopeful and searching, but now they
seemed to darken. "Yeah . . ."

"What's wrong?"

He said, "Look, Dixie. I love you. You know that.
I basically loved you the minute I met you, and I'd marry
you in a heartbeat, but . . ."

"But what?"

"I just think maybe there are a couple of reasons we shouldn't be talking about getting married right now."

"Why? What reasons?"

He let out a long sigh. "Well, for one . . . *Guidry.*"

"Guidry! What does Guidry have to do with anything?"

"Well, you have to admit, the timing is a little weird."

"What timing?"

"Umm, who got married today?"

I blinked. "Oh. *That* timing."

"Yeah."

I nodded hesitantly. "Okay. I see your point."

And I did. The timing *was* a little off. Maybe he was right. Maybe I was just being overly emotional, reacting to the stress of everything that had happened, on top of thinking about Guidry's wedding. But honestly, just between you and me, it didn't feel like that at all.

Ethan leaned in and gave me another kiss. "Let's just talk about it later."

I nodded, letting the lingering sensation of his lips on mine travel across my body like a wave. "What's the other reason?"

"Huh?"

"You said there were a *couple* reasons we shouldn't talk about getting married. What's the other one?"

There was a gleam in his eye. "Well . . . the singing."

I gave him a half grin, half grimace. "Yeah, sorry about that. How long were you listening?"

He winked. "Long enough."

"Long enough for *what*?"

"Long enough."

He pulled the curtain aside and stepped in, completely naked.

Now, normally, just the sight of Ethan's big brown eyes is enough to make me feel a little light-headed. I was thinking I should probably grab on to the towel bar just in case I keeled over, but before I got the chance, he pulled me close and wrapped his long arms around me. I melted into him, reveling in the warmth of his body against mine.

He whispered in my ear, "By the way, last time there was a rabbit by the bed. Now there's a canary on the coffee table."

I pulled back. "Yeah, wait 'til you hear what happened. I took Franklin and Gigi back home to Caroline's, and while I was there, Detective Carthage came over. He asked me if I'd walk through the Kramers' house and tell him everything I saw. I didn't want to, but I couldn't exactly say no, so then when I went over there . . ."

My voice trailed away. I noticed Ethan had lowered his chin and was staring at me with a slightly annoyed look on his face. I immediately knew what he was thinking: *"Dixie, shut the hell up."*

Well, maybe not exactly in those words—he'd never speak to me like that—but I could tell he was thinking there'd be plenty of time for talking later. The most important thing was what was happening right here . . . right now . . .

He leaned in and kissed my forehead, gently, and then he kissed my ears, and then my throat, and then he worked his way slowly around my neck and across my shoulders, all the while kneading the knots and kinks out of my back with his strong hands. The steam rose around us in little swirling clouds, filling the shower in a veil of white so thick that eventually, had anyone else been watching, they wouldn't have been able to see a single thing.

30

It had taken a lot of persuasion on my part to convince Ethan he didn't need to spend the night, especially after I'd told him about Elba Kramer. But to be honest, I wanted some time alone—some time to just sit and think about nothing. No more intrigue, no more notes, no more Elba Kramer, and no more murder. Plus, there were a lot of other things I didn't want to think about—namely, Jean Pierre Guidry, his wedding, or where he and Monistat were headed for their honeymoon . . .

I had a lot of not thinking to do.

After he left, I pulled on a pair of fleecy sweatpants, some house slippers, and a soft cotton T-shirt, and then I popped open an ice-cold Corona and headed for the hammock. On the way through the living room, I stopped to check in on Jane. I still hadn't decided if I should keep her or not, but then again I wasn't sure I had a choice. Detective Carthage had told me Elba Kramer hadn't said a word as he led her from the pool house to his car, but once inside, handcuffed and buckled in, she'd made him promise to give me a message:

Take good care of Jane.

I had draped a beach towel over her cage to help her get used to her new surroundings, and when I peeked inside, she was nestled in the far left corner, sound asleep with her beak tucked into her breast feathers.

I felt a little flutter in the center of my chest.

I'd planned on maintaining a purely business relationship with Jane. Of course, I'd do exactly as Elba Kramer had requested—find her a good home, make sure she was well cared for, etcetera—but nothing more. I wanted as few reminders as possible of everything that had happened. Only now, seeing Jane all snuggled up and content, I felt like the Grinch who stole Christmas . . . my heart was getting just a little bit bigger.

Outside, the stars were twinkling like tiny beacons in the night sky, and the waves rolling in on the beach below were sending hushed whispers through the trees. I lit one of the citronella candles we keep at the top of the steps and put it on the ice cream table by the door . . . and then my jaw dropped wide open.

Todd's old cell phone was there, right smack dab in the middle of the table with a folded note tucked underneath. I stared at it for a good ten seconds or so while all the possible explanations for how it could have gotten there ricocheted around my brain like shrapnel. Try as I might, I couldn't come up with anything good—especially given that the notes I'd received so far that week hadn't exactly been full of cheer. For a second or two, I even considered pretending I'd never seen it, but, as always, curiosity got the best of me. I slid the note out and unfolded it . . .

Hey Sis,
Paco and I got home late tonight and decided to go for a walk. You'll never believe what we found! Remember that old boat we used to play with? It was washed up on the beach right in front of the house . . . I guess now we know why you weren't answering your phone.

Love,
Michael

ps—Paco says "GPS—good thinking."

I picked up the phone and smiled as I turned it over in my hand a couple of times. Except for a couple of scratches and a few grains of sand stuck in the crevices, it seemed to have survived its ocean journey intact. Right at that very moment, as if on cue, it rang.

Without even looking, I knew it was Ethan. He'd said he'd call when he got home to make sure I hadn't changed my mind and wanted him to come back. I answered the way I imagined Billie Holiday might, puckering my lips and drawing my voice out in a velvety, high-pitched wail.

"*Helloooooo* . . ."

There was a short pause.

"Dixie, this is Samantha . . . Detective McKenzie, I mean."

"Oh my gosh! Detective McKenzie! I'm sorry, I thought you were someone else."

"Well, I'm sorry it's so late. Are you . . . drunk?"

I laughed out loud. "No! No, of course not! Well, I'm having a beer, but that's all. I swear. I was just trying to sound like Billie Holiday."

"Billie Holiday?"

"Yeah." I ducked back inside, closing the door behind me. I didn't want to make too much noise in case Michael and Paco were asleep. "It's a long story."

"Well, again, I'm sorry it's so late."

There was something in her voice that caught me off guard. For one, it was unlike Detective McKenzie to apologize for anything, especially something so trivial as a late-night phone call.

I said, "Oh, it's totally fine. I knew I'd hear from you at some point. I'm guessing Detective Carthage told you all about Elba Kramer."

"Yes . . . that's why I'm calling."

"Okay . . ."

It suddenly dawned on me that what I was hearing in her voice was sadness. A terrible thought flashed through my mind: Elba Kramer would never have allowed herself to be locked up in a jail cell like a caged animal. She was too wild for prison, too headstrong and rash, too . . . *unstable.*

I said, "Oh, no. What has she done?"

She sighed. "It's more about what she *hasn't* done. I know you're under the impression Ms. Kramer helped orchestrate the murder of those two other women, and I agree all the evidence does seem to point to that very conclusion."

I breathed a sigh of relief that Elba hadn't tried to

hurt herself. "Wait," I said. "I know what you're going to say."

"Do you?"

"Yes. You're going to say she denies knowing anything about it, but you have to trust me. She can be very convincing, and I think she's just afraid to admit she was not only involved in the murder of her husband, but those women too. And I have a pretty good feeling if you search her shop, you'll find some hat pins—the same hat pins tipped with black pearls that were found on Edith Reed and Sara Potts."

She took a deep breath. "Dixie, we've made an arrest in the murder of Elba's husband."

I nodded. "Yeah, I know. They caught him hiding in my car."

"No, I'm afraid not. The man who murdered Albert Greco was a hired assassin from Baltimore. We found him in a hospital emergency room about an hour from here, just outside Tampa."

I frowned. "Then, who . . . Wait, I don't understand."

"Dixie, when you were meeting with Ms. Kramer the day Albert Greco was gunned down, Deputy Morgan was stationed in his car outside. As soon as he heard that gunfire, he ran up to the front gate and saw a man with an automatic rifle escaping around the side of the house. Morgan immediately opened fire, but until this morning we didn't know if he hit him or not. The man we arrested outside Tampa had a bullet lodged in his right hip."

I was shaking my head. "That doesn't mean anything. How do you know . . . ?"

She interrupted. "Because we found an automatic rifle with a high-tech silencer in the trunk of the man's car, along with a file containing photos of Albert Greco, Elba Kramer's cell phone number, and a detailed blueprint of their home."

"So . . . there were *two* assassins looking for Albert Greco?"

"No. What I'm saying is that the man who murdered Edith Reed and Sara Potts had nothing to do with the assassination of Albert Greco."

I could feel my heart starting to race. I said, "No. That's impossible, because . . . because if that's true, it means somebody actually *was* trying to kill me."

There was a long pause, silent except for the sound of McKenzie's slow breathing. I could feel her waiting over the phone, waiting for me to process what she was telling me.

I said, "Look, just because you caught that gunman doesn't mean he wasn't working alone, he . . ."

"Dixie, he's confessed."

"Who?"

"The man found hiding in your car. He confessed just a short while ago. I should have called you right away, but I was hoping I could get a flight out of New Orleans and talk to you in person before . . ." She paused, searching for the right words. "I just wanted you to hear it from me before anyone else. He's confessed to the murders of Sara Potts and Edith Reed, and he's admitted that you were next."

Now, I shook my head again, this time in disbelief,

hoping at any moment I'd wake up and this whole night-mare would be over.

"Who is he?"

She hesitated. "Dixie . . . it was Morton Cobb."

I closed my eyes. "Oh, no . . ."

"Yes. Apparently, he never quite got over the scandal of being caught on that boat with Ms. Kramer. He's been plotting against everyone involved ever since . . . includ-ing you."

"You mean, because I wouldn't confiscate those tour-ists' cameras?"

"I'm sure you know it killed his career, and since then he's been in and out of at least two mental institutions. In fact, we've had our eye on Morton Cobb for quite a while. We have his phone records from that day, the day on the boat, and we believe he immediately arranged to have Elba Kramer murdered to keep her quiet, but once the newspapers published those photos the next morn-ing, he got afraid and called it off."

I closed my eyes and whispered, "I can't believe this is happening."

"And we don't know for certain it's related, but not long after the incident on the boat, Senator Cobb's wife filed for divorce, which, as I'm sure you can imagine, was not amicable. Less than a year later, her divorce attor-ney disappeared. That was nearly seven years ago, and he's still missing."

I mumbled, "Elba told me he was crazy."

"Yes. She told me Cobb never stopped harassing her, sending her rambling messages, accusing her of ruining his life, threatening revenge. In fact, she was worried he'd somehow figured out her husband's past and was planning to use it against her. That's partly why she decided to rat him out herself."

I sat down on the couch and dropped my chin to my chest. "So basically, all this time, he's been plotting his revenge."

"I'm afraid so. And there's one more thing. Elba Kramer was on Senator Cobb's hit list as well. I'm more than certain that if we hadn't arrested her, he'd have had her killed. In other words, Dixie, you saved her life."

For once, I was speechless. The idea that I'd saved Elba Kramer's life seemed beyond ridiculous, especially given the fact that she'd been so breezily willing to put my own life at risk.

McKenzie sighed. "The good news is that you won't have to worry about Senator Cobb ever again. He's in jail now, where I expect he'll be for the rest of his life."

After I rang off with McKenzie, as horrifying as the news about Senator Cobb had been, I immediately felt a sense of relief wash over me. There'd been something about Elba Kramer's story that had left me feeling uneasy, and now I knew why. She was telling the truth about Edith Reed and Sara Potts—she'd known nothing about them.

I went over and sat on the edge of the coffee table next to Jane's cage. She was in her water bowl, cheerfully splashing about and fluttering her wings, completely indifferent to the news of her former owner and not one bit shy that I'd interrupted her bath.

I said, "You know, if it hadn't been for you, this whole thing wouldn't have had such a happy ending. In fact, I'm not sure any of us would still be around to talk about it."

She plunged her head underwater and back up again, stretching her neck and puffing her feathers out like an Elizabethan ruff, then she hopped up on the lip of her bowl and blinked at me a couple of times.

It made me smile. That look in her eyes . . . I recognized it. My mind flashed back to that little sparrow I'd rescued when I was a girl, how its tiny black eyes had seemed so wise and deep, as if they somehow held all the wisdom of the world—everything that had ever happened and everything that was to come, all the twists and turns that life had in store for me.

I could hear the ocean outside, the waves rolling in like hushed breathing, as a series of images flashed through my mind—like a slide show in fast motion or a movie montage with hundreds and hundreds of pictures—my grandmother's kind eyes as she slid a plate of floppy bacon in front of me; my grandfather's hands as he showed me how to tie a Windsor knot; my mother's sewing scissors, her stern voice, her warm fingers on the back of my neck as she braided my hair; my brother's sweet smile and his baseball hat collection; my father's strong arms as he carried me up the stairs to bed—all the things I had ever loved. Ella and Billy Elliot and Charlie and Gigi and Michael and Paco and Ethan and Judy and Tanisha and Todd and Christy . . .

It's good to be alive, I thought to myself.

Just then, there was a knock on the door and I nearly

jumped out of my skin. I'd been so lost in thought I hadn't heard anyone coming up the steps, and I'd forgotten to turn the porch light on so all I could see through the glass was a looming shape, large and utterly still in the blue moonlight.

I winked at Jane. "That'll be Michael."

He'd probably seen the lights and was wondering why I was up so late, worried about me as usual. Maybe, I thought, he'd brought me a mug of hot chocolate. I rubbed my hands together excitedly as I headed for the door, thanking the powers above that I have a brother who's always looking out for me.

I turned the handle and pulled the door open.

It wasn't Michael.

The man was tall, with broad shoulders, a beaky nose, and hints of silver in his dark hair, which was disheveled and wild. He wore a white tuxedo shirt, unbuttoned at the top and wrinkled, and there were the open ends of a black bow tie dangling unevenly from his neck. Dark circles framed his desperate eyes, which were red and swollen as if he'd been crying, but there was a light in the center of his black pupils that lit a fire in the depths of my soul . . . a fire that I thought had long ago been extinguished. When I finally spoke, my voice was barely a whisper.

"Guidry . . ."

His face softened as he gave me a halfhearted smile. He said, "Surprise."